Kill Doll

Baby

Introducing Dale O'Hara,
The New Sherlock Holmes

Bobby C. McElrath

Dedication

This book is respectfully dedicated to the memory of Naomi Love McElreth. As my mother, partner, best friend, and unwavering supporter, she imparted to me the true essence of resilience.

Acknowledgment

I want to take a moment to express my heartfelt gratitude to my Lord and Savior, Jesus Christ. His unwavering guidance and support have been my anchor, especially when it came to finding the words to reach out to those who hold a special place in my heart—Virginia, Greg, Karen, Marcus, and Landin. Your belief in me is a constant source of inspiration, and I am profoundly thankful for each one of you.

To the friends who have become like family, the strangers who have offered their wisdom, and the quiet moments that have filled the pages of my journey, this book is a tapestry woven with your kindness and compassion. Your support has shown me that our stories truly do matter, and I cherish each of you dearly.

About the Author

Bobby C. McElrath faced significant challenges during his upbringing in the vibrant city of Memphis, after a good childhood in Dyersburg, Tennessee. This city, rich in musical history and culture, is marked by the struggles and triumphs of its residents. From the soulful notes of Elvis, B.B. King, and Lucille to the heartfelt redemption songs of Al Green, Dyersburg, and Memphis are places where hardship and resilience coexist, much like the grit and determination of its people. Bobby's journey reflects the complex tapestry of this unique city, highlighting both the struggles and the spirit that define it.

Despite facing numerous choices that led him to state and eventually federal prison, he found himself on a transformative path. In those challenging times, he began to use his hands and mind to seek solace in reading. With humility, he acknowledges that a greater plan was at work—a sense that God guided him to discover and appreciate the power of books, which offered him hope and wisdom during difficult moments.

In the age of social media, his progress was unstoppable. He emerged as a published author, actor, producer, director, and an exceptional master of content storytelling. Bobby's focus is on Transgressive fiction. He focuses on characters who feel confined by the norms and expectations of society and who break free of those confines in unusual or illicit ways. He has a willingness to depict forbidden behaviors and shock readers. He allows his protagonists to often pursue means to improve themselves and their surroundings, even if those means are unusual or extreme. The characters seek self-identity, inner peace, or personal freedom.

Bobby believes that writing is one of the most profound gifts bestowed upon humanity. It offers a voice to those who are often marginalized and unheard, allowing them to share their stories. Individuals who break free from the traditional constraints of taste and literary norms have a unique ability to provide powerful insights into social issues, fostering understanding and empathy in a world that often overlooks their experiences.

Bobby C. McElreth pours his heart into his creations, hoping that they will resonate with and bring comfort to everyone who encounters his work.

Prologue

As I look back over my life, if I had one thing to change about it, what would it be? The answer is nothing. My life struggles have shaped me into the woman I am today.

I wouldn't change any of it for the world! Oh, by the way. My name is Tasha Harris, but everybody calls me Doll Baby... Coming out of the trenches of West Dallas surely has its advantages and disadvantages.

Would you believe, at the age of thirteen, my own daddy pimped me out? True story. What a real jerk! Both of my parents were so far gone on crack they didn't see a damn thing wrong with pimping me out!

Just as long as they got what they wanted... I got so tired of that mess, I ran off and found myself getting into a bigger mess!

So here's my story. Enjoy...

Table of Contents

Chapter 1:
The Making Of Doll Baby
[June 1996]

Today I wanted to go and hang out with my girl Shine to celebrate my thirteenth birthday. Unfortunately, that won't be happening today thanks to my daddy Willie Fred. He made it very clear that there will be no school for me. You can just imagine how that threw me for a loop. Just when I'm going through my bad day, Shine shows up at the front door.

"What you going to do? Just keep standing there looking crazy or what?" Shine said, smiling.

Sometimes this girl knows the right things to say to make the hairs on my neck stand up.

"Come on in before your mouth drops."

"What done wrecked your nerves this morning?"

"Trust. You don't want to know."

"So they back on their bull-jive, huh?"

"You know it."

"Why you keep putting up with that crap, Doll Baby?"

"You know girlfriend, I asked myself that same question more times than I care to remember."

"Have you ever thought about putting their sorry butts in jail?"

"Wow! Snoopy Willie Fred been listening in on our conversation this whole time."

"Listen up, Shine! Or whatever your name is. Ain't nobody going nowhere but you! Now get up outta here before I make your behind sore!"

"I feel sorry for you, Doll Baby! And if you need me, just holla."

"I'm not going to tell you again! Get up outta here!"

Damn, I hate to see my girl leave. Another one of them days. Hungry and broke!

"And for you! Get yourself cleaned up. You got some work to do!"

"Where is momma Willie Fred? And don't give me that crap about you don't know!"

"Shut your sassy mouth and do what I say!"

"I'm not doing crap jack!"

That clown slapped me so hard I seen stars for a week.

It started at 11:00 a.m. and ended at 11:45 p.m. I was made to have sex with three different drug dealers and didn't receive a damn thing for my services. That was the beginning of me thinking I was losing my freaking mind. This crackhead and my moms didn't give a shit about me, and neither did I. I just wanted to talk to my girl Shine.

Let me keep it (Gangsta). That lil broad Doll Baby got the best trim on this side of the Mississippi and that's big facts... If ever a broad could break down my bankroll, she's the one for sho. Oh, by the way. I'm Silky Black. A true brick layer from the Cross Hampton's. Now, when it comes down to a woman and my money, it's no shame in my game for sho!

Okay. Since it's a mellow day out I'm going to leave the whip and hike it on down to Red's barbershop. Damn this walk have done these legs a whole lot of good. I haven't walked in years. Damn! What these niggas got going on?

A family reunion? Not a good look for me tho. Here comes these Cross Hampton Crips headed straight this way with Po'Boy leading the pack.

"Well, look at you, Silky Black. You act like you'll not that happy to see me?"

"On the real Po'Boy, I'm just here to cop a cut man."

"Ain't nothing wrong with that Playboy. Now what you been up to these days?"

"What you trying to say lil daddy?"

"You know my lil cuz Shine?"

"Yeah I know Shine. What about her?"

"Well she tells me you been poking beef into her lil friend Doll Baby. Is it true?"

What's up with this clown? All in my wax!

"Who I be poking my joint into ain't your business Po'Boy!!"

"That may be true, player, but when you go messing around with 13-year-old girls who happen to be best friends with my lil cuz, that becomes my business playboy!!"

"So what you saying?"

"This is your first and last warning to leave Doll Baby alone!!"

This boy got the game twisted for real if he thinks I'm leaving that young ass alone! But I still can't play myself. And I sure can't show no weakness.

"Like I said, Po'Boy, what I got going on with the lil broad has nothing to do with you homie!"

"Do you know what it means to have the groundhogs bring you your mail?"

"No, I don't."

"Then allow me to show you."

Damn yo! I didn't think it would come down to this! Before I could blink, Po'Boy's goons knocked me straight on my ass! I could feel the blood dripping from the right corner of my mouth. The right side of my forehead started swelling out of control. The gripping pain felt like a fat broad getting laid for the first time! I heard one of them niggas screaming: **Kill 'em Po'Boy!**

Knowing how the game is played I didn't think this nigga would pull the trigger. But I was dead wrong! He pulls up a Glock .40 and aims it right at my head, leaving a hole in my dome the size of a quarter. I guess you can say, no more trim for me...

At the age of thirteen, I should have been somewhere doing normal kid stuff. But instead, I'm somewhere having sex like a grown woman!

Then I find myself looking in the mirror asking myself, 'Is it my fault?' What a jive daddy to have in your life!

Now, if you ask me, I think he should have his throat cut! That damn Willie Fred is no damn good! And my momma ain't short stopping herself. Following this clown, Willie Fred got her on the same bull crap. I can't get a dollar from either one of them because they stay broke.

But I have so much love for my momma, though. But that Willie Fred, I don't give a rat's ass about! My mother can't love me like she wants to, because the damn crack won't let her!

"Hey, baby," Carol said with a missing tooth. "Are you still going to fix my hair today?"

"You damn right she's going to fix it!"

"I don't recall her asking you, Willie Fred!"

"Don't let your smart mouth get you knocked down this evening!"

"Leave the girl alone, Willie Fred."

"And you can just shut the hell up, too!"

"You can leave my momma alone, weak nigga!!"

I felt the bull crap coming behind those words. That sucker slapped me so hard I thought I just landed on Mars. My head was spinning out of control. I told that nigga Willie Fred that was his last time putting his hands on me!!

Chapter 2:
One Bad Bitch
[2004]

Another summer on the grind. When you been whoring as long as me and still look this good, you are one bad bitch...

One thing I know for sho. I got a body to kill for! And for any guy who wanna get down with me he better know ain't no jumping it for the free! Being pimped out by my worthless ass daddy taught me a few things. Purse first. Ass last! Everybody know that Doll Baby came straight out the trenches with a bad attitude! So to play with me is not a plus in your favor. Because in the end somebody got to win. And I never plan on losing... You see, I own the key to a sucker's heart, and that's why the average broad envy me. They'd want that status. I guess I'm going to stroll on down to the sugar shack. My girl Shine said she got a hot trick coming in tonight with a fat bankroll. Now who is calling me? My girl Shine telling me to hurry and get there before I miss out on the bankroll. When I made it inside the sugar shack, my thinking cap and my eyes were roaming all over the place looking for my girl. Damn, this place was so crowded with people I kinda got spooked for a minute.

"Damn girlfriend! You scared the hell outta me!"

"Forget that! Get yourself loose because the big bucks is on the way too hit our hands tonight."

"So who is the players?"

"You know that rich cat mister Wesley who owns all those rental properties over there on Singleton Avenue?"

"Yeah I know 'em."

"Get ready cause we'll reaching for the big cake!"

"Just make the play cause I'm with it."

"Here comes mister hot pants now with one of his associates."

"Hello, Shine? You are looking quite stunning tonight."

"Well, thank you, Mister Wesley."

"Oh! Who might this lovely specimen be?"

"I'm Doll Baby Mister Wesley."

"I'm honored to have met your acquaintance Doll Baby."

"The feeling is mutual sir."

"Do you mind if we go someplace to talk?"

"No, I don't mind Mister Wesley."

"I'm sure that Shine don't mind either?"

"No Mister Wesley, I don't mind. Me and your associate here I'm sure we will find something to get into. I'm sure you will."

I gave my girl Shine a wink before heading out the door with Mister Wesley. Riding in a brand new Lincoln did my heart a whole lot of good on this warm summer night. The thought of losing my moms several years ago keeps my heart filled with unspoken rage!

During this time four years ago, I was a fresh seventeen with the attitude of a boss bitch! This night I was up in a hotel suite grinding out with a two-thousand-dollar trick when I heard a loud pounding on the door. I jumped up with the quickness to see what the hell was going on, and the trick asking me where I'm going?

"I said, fuck man! You don't hear that loud ass banging?"

I just ignored him and went straight to the peephole and saw my girl Shine standing there, shaking out of control. When I opened the door, she rushed by me so fast I don't think she even saw the trick lying in the bed. All I knew was I had to calm her down.

"Come on Shine, and catch your breath girlfriend. Now tell me what got you all shook up?"

"Get yourself together Doll Baby, you got to come with me right now!"

"Who the hell you think you is?" the trick stated coldly. "She ain't going nowhere!"

"What you need to do is shut your fucking mouth! And keep your fat ass still! I got this lil daddy! Now, Shine, tell me what's wrong?"

"It's bad. Very bad, Doll Baby."

"Stop crying and tell me what's bad?"

"The word is out that somebody just killed your moms."

Those words just cut through me like a butcher with a dull knife ripping my insides apart. For a brief moment, I couldn't speak a word. It was like my whole world was just stripped from me.

"Where the fuck you think you'll going? You got my money. So you just going to leave like this?"

"I guess so fat ass clown!"

Me and Shine burn out in my Crown Vic making out way over to Angeline Street where we saw a lot of people standing in front of Car Daddy's trap spot.

"Say, Doll Baby, before calling the cops, I was hoping you would show up first. Go in, she's in there."

Each step that I took trying to make it to my moms, my knees felt like bricks that were weighing me down. And the only good thing about this feeling, my girl Shine was right behind me, like I knew she would. All I could think about right then was how she died because no one told me. Once we made it inside, it didn't take a rocket scientist to figure out that she was shot to death.

My momma had a hole on the right side of her head the size of a half dollar. As I looked down on my momma, I could not get a tear to drop from my eyes. That very day, I swore death on the person or persons responsible for the killing of my moms! Like I told you in the beginning, West Dallas has its advantages and disadvantages. And for my moms, she got caught up in the mix...

"I know this is a bad time for me to say this, Doll Baby, but you know I still got that case pending. When these boys show I don't want to get caught up."

"Cat Daddy, we out."

"Right on. But check it, I'm going to help out with the funeral arrangement."

"I appreciate it, but that won't be necessary. I got it Cat Daddy."
"Already. Stay strong queen."

I felt like I was leaving my moms behind. But in truth, she will always be with me because I will forever carry her in my heart... All I'm going to say about it is this, Sleep well, Momma Carol, for Baby Doll is on the move...

Old man Mister Wesley really enjoyed himself tonight after paying me a handsome amount of three bands. Of course, I put on for the cause. I wouldn't dare tell the old man this in a million years. But the truth of the matter is, he ate my pussy so good I was tempted to give him all the money back on the real...

I think the old guy got the hots for me because he already have lined up another date with me as soon as tomorrow. Oh well, what can I say? I guess your girl got it going on for sho. Or maybe you could just say, I'm one bad bitch...

Chapter 3:
Shine
[2019]

Hello everybody. I never got the chance to properly introduce myself. I'm Shine. Yes, I'm Doll Baby's best friend. I know by now you are wondering how I got the name Shine? You may not know this, but I am one year older than Doll Baby. When I was 13, she was 12. And during that time, we had somewhat of a problem. You see, growing up, I had this thing about picking on people. Especially making fun of them. But what I didn't know at the time this thing was about to change. One day, while attending Carter Middle School, this was before me and Doll Baby became friends. I saw her walking down the hallway in some ragged out clothes with her hair looking as if she hadn't combed it in years. Now the kids from around the way knew her parents was hooked on drugs which gave me more reasons to poke fun at her. Baby Doll always had the size for her age. When she passed by my hall locker, I shouted...

"Look at that nappy headed junkie!"

Before I knew it the girl knocked me flat on my back for real. That lick left me with one heck of a shiner. So now you know how I got the name...

You know I'm 37 years old now, and Doll Baby is still my best friend. The girl is a true rider. Let me tell you what went down just a week ago. On the low, I was messing around with this cat Richie Rich. A true brick layer all the way caked up and don't mind showing love with it. And that's how I got started selling work. Anyway, I was up in the Rupert Circle getting my grind on when my jive boyfriend Jack Ball pulls up with a mad look on his face.

"What you call yourself doing up here?" "What it look like I'm doing? I'm getting money?"

"You can watch your foul mouth and just tell me where you got that work from!"

"What I got going on is none of your damn business! Alright?"

"I see right now you don't hear so good. I'm going to ask you again. Where did you get that work?"

"I told you already, what I got going on is none of your damn business!"

"You think I'm playing games with you?"

"You got one second to tell me what I wanna know, or I'm going to break my foot off into a place you don't want me to!"

"I ain't scared of you fool!"

"Well you should be!"

"Forget that! I ain't got no time for your crap right now! Just go on about your business nigga and leave me alone!"

"You is my business! Now come on over here and put your mouth on this."

"What you say to me fool!"

"You heard me! Get on over here and suck on this!"

It's something wrong with this boy for real! If I had my knife I would cut his tongue straight out his mouth!

"Why don't you come over here and put your mouth on this trick! Because you sho ain't packing nothing else!"

Black as this nigga is, his face turned red like a hot pepper stuck in his ass! When I woke up in the hospital, Doll Baby was there to take me home.

That nigga Jack Ball had beat me to sleep with my left eye on swoll. A few days later I gets a call from Richie Rich telling me they'd found Jack Ball lying dead in an alley. Somebody had cut his throat. One thing for sho though, I won't be losing no sleep about it… I guess the streets gave him what he deserved (Justice).

Watch out, now I'm back on my grind, ready to shine. Just got a call from my guy, Richie Rich, letting me know he got a play for me for two ounces of hard. On the strength, he's out of town.

I'm on it like yesterday. There's something I got to be real about, and I don't say this loosely. Richie Rich don't know it, but the boy got his hooks in me. I'm talking about real deep! And I keep asking myself, what am I going to do about it? What can I do about it? Knowing that he's caught up with that airline chick. Hell, it don't matter right now anyway. Too much cake to be made. So I'm just going to keep it flowing like it's been flowing.

Damn! Who is that beating on my door like that? Oh shit! The fucking cops!

"We know you'll in there Shine, so open up!"

"Alright. Hold on a minute."

So when I opened up the door those cops looked like they'd wanted to jump me.

"Alright, what do you guys want?"

"We need for you to come with us downtown."

"Downtown for what?"

"You will be informed once we get there."

"Why can't you tell me now?"

"Once again Shine we need for you to come with us downtown."

"Am I under arrest?"

"Not yet. But if you don't come with us now you will be."

Damn! I don't have a choice. I wonder what this is about? They didn't search the crib. One thing I did notice—they'd called me by my street name.

What the hell! I can't believe this! On the way over to the precinct I'm looking out the window and what do I see? I see Richie Rich and Doll Baby going inside a motel together. The first thing that comes to my mind is what's going on? He told me he was out of town. But how can you be outta town when I see you and my best friend going inside a motel together while I'm on my way downtown to be questioned about whatever? One thing about me—I don't believe in coincidences. I believe things happen for a reason. Whatever is going on, it's not a good look…

Chapter 4:
Richie Rich

'*The World Gonna Know.*' That's my slogan for life! Have you ever wanted something so bad but knew you couldn't have it? For me to feel like this is not a good feeling at all. Oh! How rude of me. Before I give you the backstory which led me to thinking this way, here is my story.

On the night of February 9th, 1975, Barefoot gave birth to a rising star who later became known as the infallible Richie Rich… You know every hood has a story and the way you tell it, it got to be on point.

When I was born I was born on a street called Rutz Street. I had one older brother named Ced and a sister named Rika. She was in the middle and I was the baby. I went to this elementary school called C.F. Carl Elementary. Although I was a slow learner, I still had lots of friends who dug my style. What they liked the most about me is that I was always willing to listen as well as help others.

Now, one day, the teacher left her purse in the classroom, and I stole a hundred-dollar bill from it. And when lunch came around, I bought everybody in my class ice cream… And that's how I got the name Richie Rich…

They were transporting the Black and Mexican kids from West and North Dallas to the middle schools based on their race. All my friends ended up returning to West Dallas (Edison M.S.).

Being one of the remaining kids from West Dallas, Franklin was normal for me because I enjoyed their curriculum and the many opportunities afforded to me at Franklin Middle School.

When I had finished the 8th grade, instead of me going to the high school across the street, I ended up finishing my grade school year at Pinkston in West Dallas.

After dropping out of school in my 11th year, all I could think about was the money. That led me to believe one day I would be the next Floyd Mayweather of boxing because I was damn good at it!

After copping a job at a local Burger King, I would go train at Wesley Franklin's gym 5 days a week after work. I got so good with this boxing thing it was now time for me to box Golden Gloves.

Now, one day, the coach had a sit-down with the team of boxers and made it clear that I had real potential to become a great boxer. But the word got out that I was messing around too much with this girl, and the coach didn't like it. I was 17 and in love at the time. What a combination!

The coach told me I had a choice to make. Either to box or continue to play around with this girl. So I chose the girl. And that was the worst mistake I ever made! This girl I had chosen over my boxing career left me for my cousin, and 9 months later, she is pregnant!

That was one blow I could not take on the chin…

From that day forward, I decided to harden my heart like an Egyptian King. When it came down to a woman, there was no trust in it… I was so messed up behind what my cousin had done, I wanted to touch him on sight! But being the boss that I am, I just let it go.

I could not believe the things that were going on in my life. Trying to get over one thing, and here comes another one.

My best friend Lil Rob was living in St. Louis now. One day, he called me and asked if I could come to St. Louis and help him out at the boys' club?
He had several young boys he was training to box. Now he knew I had a lot of training myself in the field of boxing. So on my way there, the news got around that Rob had been murdered. Somebody snuck through the window and shot him between the eyes.

That situation changed my life forever. Now I was truly a man on a mission…

I was walking home one day when this cat Pokey pulls up.

"My man Richie Rich. I got to lay something on you A.S.A.P. Your name is ringing louder than a wedding bell on these streets lil homie!"

"What you mean playboy?"

"Don't play me like that! You know where I'm coming from. Now how would you like running your side of town?"

"Come on now you know I'm with that."

So we hopped in his car and drove to the projects known as the *(Fish Trap)*.

The Fish Trap was known for housing the Fish Trap Bloods. During this time I was not associated with any street gang. All my cousins had ties with the Crips. Oh, I forgot to mention, Pokey is my cousin and he's Blood. There is something that I seem to notice from around the way is that all the honey's want to cater to the street thugs. And to see that, got me to thinking about joining forces with my cousin Pokey.

While we were in the car talking, he told me the way I trap, plus not being affiliated, I could take over my side of town. Hey! Let's not get it twisted. In truth, he wanted to do it himself, but being affiliated the fighting and drugs don't mix!

So, being the person I am, I agreed to carry out the business at Cross Hampton…

Cuz dropped me back off at the crib, then popped the trunk. Low and behold it was a dope boy dream to see the work that ole Pokey had. My eyes lit up like a bolt of lightning coming straight out the heavens… I was so caught up in the moment to get down to business, I totally forgot this block had the notorious Rolling 60's name on it! This shit just got real and fast...

As I approached the block, I saw a large crowd looking at me. They ran up to see who I was.

"Yo homie! Do you know where you at cuz?"

The reason I wasn't recognized by them—I had on all this red on a Crip set. The money had me tripping for sho.

"Yo Blacc, that's Richie Rich in all that red!"

"Yo, cuz we already know how you get down, so you get a free pass on this one. Now if you want to continue to work our block you got to drop the red and crip the blue you feel me?"

Now, Blacc was not the type to play around with so I gave it to him on the real.

"Man you know I respect the game. And you know I'm all about the paper. So whatever it take I'm with it for sho."

"Good. Tomorrow we gonna put you down so sleep tight and keep it gutta!"

"I got cha Blacc!"

"Right on. I'll get up with you tomorrow."

All night long, the only thing I could think about was getting blessed into the set. But you know in life, sometimes you got to give something in order to get something. And that something for me was the money…

But I'm no fool in my thinking, though. Everything comes with a price. And what about tomorrow? Will I have to pay some dues? And if so, what will it be?

Taking care of this business is something ole Pokey is not going to be in tune with.

Boy don't I got it coming from him. But I'm sure that's not going to stop anything because Pokey is definitely about the paper.

Right now I just got a lot on my mind so the best thing I can do right now is go chill at my spot for a minute and grab me a fine thick honey and lay back…

Damn yo! I wasn't at the crib a hot minute before I hear a loud banging at the door! It was one of the Rolling 60's. That crazy ass nigga Damn Fool!

"What's up, money?"

"Bring your ass out here so I can talk to you!"

"Alright. What's up?"

"Didn't I tell you about selling your work around here with all that red on? Don't you know this is Crip Nation?"

"I guess you haven't talked to Blacc yet?"

"What you mean?"

"I already have spoken with Blacc about this. And we have made time for tomorrow to put me down."

"So what you are telling me is that you and Blacc have made a decision without telling me about it?"

"For real though, I thought he have spoken to you about it."

"And besides that I didn't think I was doing anything wrong on the strength of Barefoot."

"I don't care who your momma is! Ain't no tomorrow! It's going down today!
Or you can take your ass right on back over to the projects! I got to be real with you. This nigga was scaring the hell out of me!

"Alright Damn Fool. I'm with it."

"Stay put. A couple of the guys is going to pick you up in about an hour."

Now I'm sitting here wondering what the fuck! The power of money can blow your freaking mind!

Oh what a web I just weaved…

My crib on Toronto Street was also my trap spot. This street was all the way live for sho!

Anything you wanted was on this block including some of the baddest honey's from around the way.

Now there was this one chick a lot of the G's took notice too.

She went by the name Doll Baby. And when you see her beautiful face it reminds you of a doll.

In truth I've been captivated by her beauty for a minute.

Wishing many nights I could lay between those thick yellow legs…

If you saw her in rare form then you would know what I mean.

Even some women want a taste of this Doll Baby.

Oh I see they'd made it. It was now 2:00 o'clock on the dot Saturday on the p.m. It was my man Blacc rolling up in a 1999 Cutless Supreme with two of the homies with him.

"Get in you know what it was cuz! We about to see where your heart is lil nigga. Once we cross this bridge ain't no turning back!"

Blacc told me to listen what Damn Fool said and don't say nothing! Damn Fool was sipping on some old Canadian whiskey talking shit at me.

"Since you want to live off the rep of your momma, it's time for you to make a name for your damn self! I be damn if I keep letting anybody wear red on my set!"

When I was looking down at the floorboard of the seat, I saw enough guns to take the city to war. So I asked them what we gonna do with all of that?

"We'll going on a hoo ride out in the Frazier Courts," Blacc said.

"What we going there for?"

"Keep your mouth shut and listen to what Damn Fool got to say about it! Because if you don't this could become your burial ground!"

"Once we go over the bridge there will be 4 or 5 dudes in red standing around or sitting on the green box. This is Damn Fool talking. I want you to scream out CHC bitch!"

That's when Damn Fool hand me a gauge taped in blue and from that point on all you could hear was the sound of gun fire erupting! Right after the shooting Damn Fool hand me a blunt and said he was proud of me. After leaving Burger King we were headed back to West Dallas because it was now time for them to jump me in. When getting out the car at the detail shop 6 gang members approached me asking was I ready to be put down? And before I could give a reply one of the 6 took off on me with great speed! Leaving my head ringing like a 50 ton bell! What troubled me the most—I couldn't fight back! I had to endure a sixty second ass whipping that left the side of my head on swoll...

I was told by Damn Fool, once I was back on the block he wanted to see me in blue! And that what it was cuz!

Now sit back and relax, and continue enjoying the story because you haven't heard the last of Richie Rich and Doll Baby...

Chapter 5:
Doll Baby / The Life Of A Hustler

The sun was at its highest peak today (12 o'clock noon), with the temperature of about 98 degrees, with an index of about 107. There was not an inch of wind blowing anywhere except in my apartment. And if it wasn't for the fact that I'm about to make some big chips, I wouldn't leave this apartment for the rest of the day... But what do I have to complain about?

This old trick, Mister Wesley sure knows how to reel me in—that's for sho. A damn good paymaster. My very own slot machine... if you know what I mean?

What the hell! Some niggas just busted in on me! It's that crazy ass nigga Damn Fool!

"Sit your bottom down, Doll Baby!"

"What the hell is wrong with you niggas busting in on me like that!"

"I won't tell you again to sit your ass down, Doll Baby!"

That crazy look Damn Fool had in his eyes made it clear for me to sit my ass right on down with no hesitation. Now whatever was going on— it wasn't a good look...

"Now that I'm seated, do you mind telling me what the hell is going on?"

"That's what I'm here for. Now check this... That sucker boy you been playing around with have stepped his ass into some tall shit this time!"

"And who might that sucker boy be? Well—I'm waiting?"

"If you didn't have such a pretty face I would bust it up right now for playing games!"

"Alright Damn Fool! Just make your point!"

"Do you know who Don Pomlerro is? Hell! You might done fucked him a couple of times already!"

"Who I fuck nigga is none of your damn business!!!"

"Sho you right. Now let's get back to the business! Do you know Don Pomlerro?"

"Yea, I heard a few things about 'em. Why?"

"Word on the streets say, your boy Easy is a government rat who works for the feds. And to top that off the nigga hit one of Don Pomlerro's stash spots for 40 bricks of dogg food!"

"Okay. But what that got to do with me though?"

"You ask the Don that!"

"I'm not asking him shit!"

"That's what you think! Now get your wide ass up and let's roll before I slap your freaking head off!"

"Yea right! Getting up is not the problem but rolling with you nigga, now that's a problem!"

When I stood up to adjust my skirt, I just knew I had the situation under control… until Damn Fool showed me different. That clown slaps me back onto the couch, leaving me with a mild headache and a slight toothache…

By this time, I wanted to kill this fool! But I was wrapped up in a no-win situation for the moment. The nigga goons were on high alert! So I knew I had to calm myself down before this fool took action again.

He reaches down and grabs my arm, pulling me to my feet, leaving a bruise on the damn thing! What a jerk! How about the fool got the nerve to kiss me!

His breath was so foul it almost cut straight through my thin ass skirt. The next thing I knew, I was on my way to see Don Pomlerro…

My eyes were in awe. Damn, this dude got a fat crib! The way I was looking, he found a way to break the ice.

"Ms. Doll Baby, I can see that you are kind of intrigued with my home."

"Yes I am Don Pomlerro."

"Allow me to give you a tour of the place?"

"I think I would like that."

As we were walking the grounds of his beautiful mansion, hidden, but not secluded. I saw a large backyard with sandstone patios, multi-leveled swimming and heated pools, with a small waterfall leading into a koi-pond decked with all the bamboo and algae covered rocks...

And when I layed eyes on the large Persian rug I ask could I take my shoes off? And of course he said yes. After the beautiful tour he had given me things went straight back to business as if he had just done nothing.

"Ms. Doll Baby? Do you really know who I am?"

"I think so."

"Do you know why you are here?"

"I got a slight idea about it."

"Good. Now since you got a slight idea, would you be willing to help me with a slight problem if the price is right?"

"It depends."

"Meaning?"

"Depending on what the slight problem is."

"How long have you been fooling around with this boy Easy?"

"With all due respect, Don Pomlerro, who I be fooling around with is my business, sir, not yours."

"You know, Doll Baby, I've heard some pretty good things about you. Especially the part about how smart you are. Is that true?"

"Don Pomlerro, could you please just cut through the jive and tell me where you are going with this?"

"If you are a smart woman, like I think you are, then you should know I'm not the playing type! This boy, Easy, must die! And will die! And you'll going to help me accomplish this!!"

My stomach had so many butterflies in it I thought I was about to have a nervous breakdown because of all this pressure! Hell!! Look at what the man did to Big Bleep when Bleep tryed to play 'em!

A couple of years back Big Bleep came up quick in the heroin game when he got out the feds. When he was in the feds, he met Adonis Pomlerro, the brother of Don Pomlerro, and that's how he came up so fast. But like all good hustlers they'd got one thing in common (A Habit).

You see, instead of Big Bleep taking Don Pomlerro his money for the drugs he sold he decides to mess it off with the hoes and the gambling think—...ing that he had it made because of Adonis. But when Don Pomlerro found out about what he had done, he sent for his brother Joey and had him to bring Big Bleep to one of his trap spots.

It was said that when Big Bleep laid his eyes on Don Pomlerro, he immediately started pissing on himself...

Joey wrapped a rope around his neck and that's when Don Pomlerro sliced his throat from ear to ear as he watched Big Bleep body fall to the pavement with no remorse...

At this point I'm not giving a damn about no Don Pomlerro! But I did tell the man I would help him out. But first I got to make a run...

This is your boy Easy. Hold on a minute I got to take this call from my man Richie Rich.

What's popping cuz?"

"Man, I just got this crazy call from Doll Baby saying, that you and me should leave the set for a few hours:"

"She didn't give you no reason why?"

"Nah. Just said basically that we should burn out for a minute."

"How did she say it?"

"What you mean how she said it?"

"Did she say it like she was excited or what?"

"Nah. She was mellow with it tho."

"So what you think?"

"I don't know. But I can tell you this, she didn't say it for no reason!"

"Sho you right. One thing about this chick she gonna keep it G on some real shit!"

"Already."

"I think I'm just gonna burn out just to see what the play is."

"Yo lil daddy, swing by here and bring me a band. I'll give it back later in the night."

"I got cha. Just give me a minute…"

Here I am again ole Richie Rich chilling at the trap counting big faces while my trap phone is jumping like a virgin scared of the big boy!

After two hours of making it do what it do, I get a call on my private phone from one of the homies informing me of what just went down on VilBig Rd.

It was said that Damn Fool had a big crap game going on in the VilBig. All the top players and hustlers were there getting their bets on. As you know Damn Fool was calling the shots in the place. The apartment was jammed packed with about half a mill to win…

A few of the bitches was coming in and out serving the players drinks, and on a few occasion, ready to shake it up for the crew.

Now in the beginning of the game it started out with bet a hundred and shoot a hundred. But that didn't last long after about an hour into the game. It was now bet a thousand, hit a thousand.

As the room temperature was about 70 degrees you could see the sweat forming on top of Damn Fool's forehead after looking down at the pool table which contained 60 bands betted on a four.

After catching a four for a point, Damn Fool next shot was a six. Clearing his throat and wiping the sweat from his forehead his second shot was a crap. It was so quiet in the place you could hear a tear drop falling to the floor.

And right before he released the dice on his third shot one of the bitches screamed out!

Hit nigga! Oh my!

When the dice stopped spinning the number was four tray...

And when it was said the boy Damn Fool went over the edge, that was putting it mildly.

The broad that screamed out when Damn Fool threw the dice, in his crazy way of thinking he did the woman real ugly… After dragging her outside with her face already busted up, he begins to stomp her out! What a jerk! No one tried to help this woman because they'd were afraid of this clown Damn Fool! But suddenly, without warning, it appeared that time had stopped for a brief second. There was not a crisp of wind in sight; when the hooded stranger kept creeping up behind Damn Fool with the precision of a starving predator. The people who were standing around were anticipating perhaps more action was well on the way. There was a woman who screamed out!

"Look at that maniac and what he is doing to that poor girl!!!"

There was not one sympathetic current running through his body… This cold-hearted monster perpetrated this malicious assault against this woman because he felt she was the cause of him losing his money. He never even considered it was his own dumb ass fault! But anyway, the hooded predator made his way up on Damn Fool without him noticing it. While Damn Fool was looking down at the woman he almost beat to death, he never heard the sounds that took his life.

The predator held a short-barreled .357 Magnum with hollow tips in his right hand, pointed at the back of Damn Fool's head. Two shots ripped the back of his head out before hitting the ground! The woman lying still on the ground won't be the only one to be rushed to the hospital…

I had to call Easy back over to the crib A.S.A.P. because the news about Damn Fool was spreading like a wild fire. And besides that Doll Baby wanted to get up with me and Easy. When her fine ass first came through the door I wasted no time getting to the issue.

"Do you mind telling us what happened to Damn Fool?"

"Why you asking me? I'm not here for that!"

"Doll Baby, Easy said calmly. We need some answers fast! This shit's about to get out of hand real fast!"

"I'll give you that, because you'll right! It's about to get real ugly for you Easy!"

"When you say shit like that, Doll Baby, don't keep me hanging! Give me the straight spill!"

"Alright. Now, before Damn Fool went and got himself all wacked out, him and a few of his goonies paid me a visit, which wasn't a pleasant one. And basically, the conversation was about you, Easy. Let me just cut through the bone and get to the meat. They'd drove me to the mansion of Don Pomlerro. When I got there, Pomlerro instructed them to leave. The Don didn't play around. He told me you were a rat working for the feds who robbed one of his stash spots for 45 bricks of heroin. He said you must die and will die!

He went on to say, he wanted me to help him. But right now all I wanna know is it true?"

"Yes and no. The part about me being a fed rat, that's not true. Busting his ass for them 40 bricks, now that's true.

"You know I believe you Easy, Richie Rich said. But that's not the thing. The thing is, we got a deadly thorn in our side that need to be removed!"

"I feel you on that, bruh. But who's going to do the removing?"

"Listen up, fellows. Since we are in this thing together, I think it's time to come up with a plan to meet the needs of Don Pomlerro. Because if not, my career as a hustler is over, and I can't stand that!"

"Doll Baby," Richie Rich said, "Let me ask you something?"

"What you waiting for? Ask away?"

"Before Damn Fool was killed you called me and said to me get up with Easy and let him know we both should get off the set for a minute. You knew something was about to go down, didn't you? My other question to you is this. Did you kill Damn Fool!?!?

Chapter 6:
No Love For Daddy

There I was lying in bed inside my brand new home, Mr. Wesley bought for me. Thinking back 15 years ago, when my mother was killed. And right now I wanna get drunk just to erase the pain I feel for her. Regardless of what she did or how she did it, that was still my momma!

Well, to ease my mind a little, I got a date with my girl Shine after she finishes up with her money man. Since it ain't nothing for me to do right now, I might as well blow me a blunt to get myself in the mood for whatever… Now smoking too much of this shit makes me have nightmares. So I got to be careful with it. Not only that tho. The shit makes me horny as hell! And that's not good for the business I'm into…

It seems like every time I'm in the mood to get lost in myself this damn phone starts ringing! Hell! I can't catch a break! Why is Shine calling me? It's not time for us to get up yet?

"What's up Shine? I know it's not time for us to get up yet?"

"Girl listen to me! I just found out something from my money man that you need to know about like right now!"

"I tell you what! It better be worth my time or I'm going to wrap that ass up!"

"I jive you not, Doll Baby! This is some real news you wanna hear about."

"I can hear it in your voice, whatever you heard it got to be solid."

"As a rock girlfriend!"

"Okay. Who's meeting who?"

"I'll be there within the hour."

"Can't wait to hear the good news."

"I don't know about all of that. But what I do know it's some news to die for…

Now by the time Shine made it over I was good and high on this popcorn cush ready to hear what she had to say.

"You sho know what to say, cause I sho need it!"

The girl wasn't lying. And all I can say, the chick got the lungs of a steel tank.

"Earlier on the phone you had a lot to say. Now say what it is that you came here to say."

"Give me a minute girl this is some good cush."

As I watched Shine take the last puff of the cush blunt she gave me this look I have never seen before. To me it was the look of lust. This girl already know I don't swing like that for the free and I hope she don't try me like that either.

"Shine I think you need to catch up with your thinking and tell me what the hell is going on!"

Although I'm still good and high, I don't have a thing for a woman…

"Doll Baby, tighten up your seat belt sugar because you'll not going to dig this ride. You see girl, my money man told me the killing of your mother was a mistake."

"What the hell you mean! A mistake!"

"Slow down Doll Baby and let me make it clear for you. You remember when…

Po'Boys car got hit for those ten birds?"

"That was 15 years ago but I do remember some talk about it."

"Well anyway my money man told me it was your daddy who told Po'Boy your momma was the one who pilled him for the birds."

"Your money man what's his name?"

"They call him Gangsta Bo."

"This Gangsta Bo seem to know a lot about what went on with my momma?"

"Brace yourself for this one Doll Baby because you'll right! It was my money man who killed your mother on the order of Po'Boy."

"And how long have you known this shit!"

"Just like I told you! I just found out about it myself."

"That low down piece of shit! Junkie ass nigga sold my old bird out for some fucking crumbs!"

"I can just imagine how you feel right now Doll Baby."

"I don't think so. But anyway, since your money man played a big part in all of this, how you suppose we handle it?"

"The way I see it, start with the one who put the order in!"

"Sho you right! That's just what we gonna do!"

It's been about two months since Shine told me what happened to my mother. And since today is Shine's birthday I thought it would be a good idea just to focus on her. This crazy girl seemed to have invited everybody in the neighborhood to the party—including her small pitbull (Rex), who enjoys tearing up everything in his sight. Shine loves Rex so much when she saw a small cut on his paw she started crying. But that's my girl tho… And of course Po'boy and Gangsta Bo payed for everything. Oh here comes Shine.

"Nice party ain't it girl?"

"Yes it is Shine. Yes it is."

"This is the first time I've ever seen the Crips and Bloods come together without there being bloodshed."

"Especially on this crazy ass street (Rutz)."

"You know the boy Po'boy been asking about you Doll Baby?"

"Asking about me for what?"

"You already know he wanna get with you. And I can see it in your eyes, the evil behind the stare."

"I don't know what you're talking about. I look like this all the time."

"Don't run that smack on me! You and I both know what it is, girlfriend!"

"Instead of you busting my chops, could you just go and get me a drink?"

While Shine went to get me a drink, I noticed Po'boy inching his way over to me. I can't lie, the boy was looking like a million for sho!

"What's up Po'boy? Look like you got something on your mind?"

"Not really. I just saw your fine self over here that's all."

"Where is your lady friend? I don't see her at the party?"

"Who knows? Somewhere with her mouth full, you feel me?"

"That's what you think of every lady you involve yourself with?"

"Yes if she play herself like that!"

"So what do you think of me?"

"One thing about you, Doll Baby, you'll going to keep it 100 all the way around the board!"

"I know you didn't just come over here for small talk. So what's on your mind?"

"What's the ticket for tonight?"

"It depends on what you want."

"I want the whole 9."

"Cool. Three bands will fit the bill."

"Right on. Just name the time and the spot."

"The time is 10 p.m. You name the place.?"

"I'm going to rent a suite at the Antoe (Hotel) for us tonight. You will know the room number. And if I'm not there by ten just go on in."

"I got cha."

Dear readers, this is Po'Boy talking. You already know I got a hot date with bad ass Doll Baby? I been wanting to get it in with her for a minute you know? But believe it or not, to connect with this chick your paper got to be right. Because that's the only thing this girl lives for is the paper! Let me see who this is banging at my freaking door!

"What's up with you Gangsta Bo? Banging on my door like that!"

"I had to see you homie A.S.A.P."

"Hell! You could have used the damn phone!"

"It didn't matter. I was already here."

"Fuck that! What's on your mind chief?"

"Bruh. I know you'll about to get your serve on with Doll Baby right?"

"You know it!"

"I don't think that's a good idea bruh."

"And why not?"

"I think she's trying to set you up for real!"

"And why do you think that?"

"Listen bruh. A few months ago I made a dumb move with this girl Shine. One night I was good and high after knocking her off. I guess my conscious got the best of me. I told her the whole story of why Doll Baby's momma was killed."

"…got the best of me. I told her the whole story of why Doll Baby's momma was killed."

"You did what nigga!"

"You heard me! Doll Baby know you ordered the sauce for her momma!"

"Why is you just now telling me this shit!"

"I don't know Po'Boy."

"What I do know is this! We got a big problem for sho! Check this. Right after I drop the big boy into that load Doll Baby got to go without question! And you'll going to make it all happen my guy!"

"What you want me to do?"

"At 9:15 p.m.. Bring me that .357 with the silencer and meet me at the trap in Rupert Circle. And don't be late!"

"I got cha bruh."

Just like clock work Gangsta Bo was right on time with .357 magnum in his right hand with the silencer laced around the barrel. When Po'Boy saw him he begin to make his way towards him in such a hurry that one could see the deadly venom in his eyes that would have made a silver-back to take flight! A slight breeze were blowing in the crisp night air as Po'Boy slowly turned down his pace while approaching Gangsta Bo with confidence and rage!

After this night, there will be no rules to the game… Exhilarated by the sleek look in his eyes, Po'Boy screamed at Gangsta Bo to reach him the gun! Being in compliance, Gangsta Bo followed Po'Boy's instructions that led to a new phase. At the funeral, Po'Boy had to have a closed casket because those 2 shots from Gangsta Bo's gun ripped his entire face apart! Lying dead on the pavement, the fiends goes deep inside Po'Boy's pockets in hope to find anything to get high.

Meanwhile, over at the Antoe Hotel, Shine was lying in bed when Gangsta Bo entered the room with this satisfying look on his face as if to say, I told ya! Before crawling in between the sheets with Shine, she hands him a bag of money that came from Doll Baby for putting in such fine work. Now, right when Gangsta Bo was just about ready to enter Shine's delicate cat all hell broke loose: when that extra large Bolivian knife struck his jugular vein which caused him to bleed out within minutes… Oh my! The life inside of West Dallas!

Now it could be said that pussy brought you in and pussy took you out! Hold what you got. We can't forget about old Willie Fred now.

3 weeks after the death of Po'Boy and Gangsta Bo, Willie Fred died from a hot shot after he thought it was heroin (Battery acid)… I guess you could… say, there was no love for Willie Fred…

Chapter 7:
Old Mr. Wesley

Greetings everyone. My name is Wesley, but everyone calls me Mr. Wesley.

And by the way, I'm rich. But to look at me, you wouldn't know it because I'm not your average white guy with money who runs around letting the world know I got it unless she's beautiful and I want her! Now, in the case of Doll Baby, I want her, and I will do whatever it takes to keep her! She is one special cookie... I have never felt this way about a black woman in my entire life until I met Doll Baby! Yes. I know what she does for a living, and I assure you that do not matter to me whatsoever! That ex-wife of mine never made me feel this good! Oh I forgot. I got a hot date at ten with you know who... See you guys later...

After sitting back, preparing myself for my date with Mr. Wesley, I have this flash back that takes me to the year 1999. This was a situation that occurred three days after my 16th birthday. It was on a warm Saturday afternoon, the park was jumping out of control with many of the dope boys and players out dressed to impress. All the ladies had on their latest gear, with rings on every finger and the loop earrings to match. The latest attraction was basketball star Peevy, along with his girlfriend Devin. Now, let me give you a little spill about Devin. You know West Dallas is known for its fight game. Now Devin was the neighborhood bully who felt like she could beat up every female, including some males. The buzz around the city was that Devin was going to lay lands on me when she caught up with me! So when she approached me that day in the park, everybody automatically assumed Devin was going to beat me down. But what some of the people didn't know was that I was the only girl in West Dallas who trained at the boys' club. But anyway, the bets were on. Check this! The majority of those high-profile dope boys were betting big bucks on Devin to beat me out.

Over by the famous pool site where everybody put down there fight game, Devin pulls up with her crew giving me the evil eye like I cared about that!

"What is your damn problem! Trying to pull up on my man?"

Devin's crew started chanting, "You better watch your man around Doll Baby."

"You can slow your roll, Devin, because I'm not the one you need to be checking for real!!"

"You can stop running, game bitch! Peevy already told me what your grimmy ass was up to a couple of weeks ago!!"

"So what did you tell this silly bitch! Peevy?"

"Just what it was. You tried to get me to have sex with you."

"And so this dumb ass bitch believe that?"

"If you call me one more bitch! I'm gonna lose my foot off into your wide ass!"

"I'm telling you right now, Devin, I'm not one of your flunkies you can run that game on. I'm going to beat the shit outta you if you dip this way!"

When everybody got to laughing Devin made her move at me. When she made her move toward me I lost all sense of directions in a hurry! I sprung into action like a professional boxer with nothing to lose but get in a bitch ass throwing everything I got! With the speed of lightning, I snatched Devin by the hair, pulling her head downward by her braids, leaving her face wide open for my knee to have its way! A shocking moan escaped from her lips as I dropped her to the pavement! Don't you guys trip on me because I'm only giving this tramp what she's been itching for... How in the hell is a hooker like me gonna get caught up with a trick like Peevy? Back to work. When Devin came back to her senses, she stood up and lunged forward at me in full force! But what that did was outrage me! As I positioned myself to fight, I began to deliver a forceful strike against Devin's face with blow after blow, operating on her face with such sufficiency that one would assume I was a licensed surgeon! Dazed and confused, this bitch was barely able to stand! She was still on her feet until I hit her across the jaw with a hard right. All I could say was out for the count when the crowd started screaming for someone to bring a bucket of water... Maybe next time this clown will stay in her place and leave a bitch like me alone!

I know damn well, this can't be Mr. Wesley: ringing the doorbell! And if it is this man got it bad for sho. I haven't even finished grooming the cat yet. But anyway, let me check and see who this is. Damn! It's the boy Easy. I can't lie tho, the boy is definitely fine with a fat bank, you feel me? I know you do. You know the boy has got real potential to become a real force in this drug game. Plus, he got a hot thing for me, which is not a plus in his favor. He's no match for me. When you have lived the life I have lived. You learn a lot from the game... And trying to wife me up is not part of it! I guess I'll be killing two birds at different times...

"What's wrong with you ringing my doorbell like that?"

"Have you forgot we got a date tonight?"

"I told you on the 17th."

"What you think the day is?"

"I be damn! You are right. How could I forget the time of day like that?"

"It's not a big thing, Doll Baby. Do what you gotta do. I'll just sit here and chill until you're done with your grooming."

"What you know about a hoe grooming lil fellow?"

"Come on, Doll Baby. How many times I got to tell you not to call me lil fellow?"

"Alright big man just give me a minute."

Considering all the other guys I've been with, I have to admit I got a special liking for Easy. But of course, I could never show my real feelings because that's not part of the game. And besides that, these cold-hearted bitches would never let me live it down knowing I caught a buzz from a trick! Instead of the paper!

"I got to give you your props, Doll Baby, you look good enough to eat!"

"Shell told me you'll be about to make a big play tonight. Is that true?"

"What's true that fast talking sister of mine don't know how to keep her trap shut!"

"Come on, Easy give the girl a break. You already know she's my round."

"Let me ask you something, Doll Baby?"

"What you waiting for?"

"When did you start messing around with Richie Rich?"

"Lets get something straight right now Easy! Who I mess around with don't concern you. So stick to the script!

"True that. So whats it going to cost me this time?"

"For dipping in my business three bands will be the ticket for tonight!"

"Hey, lady, turn that up a minute! It's that crooked ass Mayor Griswall up for re-election again. Somebody need to off that chump for real! He want to make all the money and make it hard on the players if they don't come through for him. Fuck that clown!"

"Stop that, Easy! Mayor Driswall is my money man."

"Damn Doll Baby! How many money men do you have, girl?"

"That's for me to know and for you to find out if you wanna know. Now what you got planned for us?"

"I got to put that on hold for a sec. The reason being I need your help with something."

"And what might that something be?"

"I got to wrap up two hundred bands for the work, and I need your help doing it."

"You know I don't mind helping you, sugar."

"Can I be real with you, Doll Baby?"

"You sure can."

"Now I don't want to come off sounding like a real sucker, you dig? But here's the spill. I got this thing for you to the point I can't shake it.

Over time in my life, I have put in a lot of work, paying my dues to the game, and stood strong through it all. But now I feel like a wounded animal who can't fend for himself, knowing I could never have you completely. How can a man in my position could have these type S of feelings for a hooker?"

"Oh, Easy baby! That is about the sweetest thing a man has ever said to me.

"But it's true, tho. And my silly ass sister think it's funny because I got this thing for you!"

"But what about that crazy girlfriend you got? What's her name?"

"Forget that! Shonda don't want a damn thing from me except the paper! Building some type of relationship with her is an absolute no, no!"

"So you think you can build one with me?"

"I would like to think so."

"!You don't think it would get in the way of your money?"

"I don't see why it should. And with you by my side, we can get this paper together, you feel me?"

"Right now, that's a lot for me to take in."

"How bout I make love to you? That will give you something else to think about."

"We can make it happen, but not here. And add a fifty to those three bands."

"Why?"

"Because I want a bottle of that female notta that have me cumming everywhere."

"Sho, you right!"

Old Mr. Wesley was in a very good mood as he drove his brand new Lincoln Town car in hot pursuit of the one woman whom he had secretly fallen in love with. The only woman on earth who knows how to make his toes curl...

Turning off an intersection onto a red light, Mr. Wesley saw a familiar face getting out of a light blue charger, heading inside of a hotel. The man he saw, he did not recognize, but the woman he did. So Mr. Wesley decided to head over to the hotel to investigate. Now the obvious was clear. What he saw was eating at his insides like cancer! Wondering why she would do him like that, knowing he had a date with her?

When he walked up to the desk clerk Mr. Wesley kept his composure. He gave a description of the couple and asked for their room number. And when the clerk declined to give him the info he handed her two one hundred dollar bills, and the rest was history...

After standing at their room door for the last 10 minutes, hearing the soft moans coming from Doll Baby making love to the stranger, sent his mind into oblivion.

I can't accept this! And I will never accept it! Who in the hell do she think I am! Do she think she's going to get away with this crap! I should hope not? And for that young fool she's been playing around with! I will pay him a visit real soon! You can count on it... Don't they know that the wages of sin is death? I got to make a phone call.

"Hello?"

"Yes. This is Mr. Wesley. I need to see you in a hurry."

"I will be around your way within the hour."

"Good."

Chapter 8:
Greed Kills

Don Pomlerro sit inside his illustrious study going over a few things in his mind pertaining to Mayor Driswall and why his operations inside West Dallas is being disrespected by the Crips and Bloods?

I have paid this fool Griswall good money to keep the product flowing throughout West Dallas! But unfortunately for me that's not the case. What I been hearing, the Crips and Bloods have muscled their way into my territory taking control over a few of my important sites! Now I have to wonder if Driswall have made a deal with them? And to top that off this chick Doll Baby is all over the place fucking around with a lot of the big players! What is her angle? And what do she know? And if she don't set the play for this boy

Easy, real soon, she can cancel her whore game permanently! Hold on I got to take this call.

"Right. I'm on the way."

I called for my driver to get the car ready. And when we pulls up in front of Mr. Wesley's front gate we were met by a huge full grown great dane just looking to tear into somebody's ass!

"Sibble, get back, girl! Mr. Wesley shouted!

For a brief moment, ole Sibble acted like she had a hearing problem.

"Come with me, gentlemen. And for you, Sibble, go to your hut now!

One could see that the hut was a form of punishment for Sibble. With her head down she followed Mr. Wesley's orders. He then preceded to walk us around to an area that was not connected to his house. From the outside structure it looks like a common shed. But on the inside, it puts you in the mind-set of a command station preparing for war.

Computers and maps were neatly in place, filled with pure intelligence, and a long, glossy oak wood table with a stack of papers in front of him.

"Take your seats, gentlemen. Don Pomlerro, are you aware we have some serious problems going on in West Dallas?"

"Yes, Mr. Wesley. And I do agree."

"Don Pomlerro, there is a situation that need my immediate attention and I'd would like for you to look into it for me."

"And what might that be, sir?"

"Find out who is this trouble maker fooling around with Doll Baby!"

"I'd think I already know who it is, Mr. Wesley."

"So, do you mind telling me who the troublemaker is?"

"He goes by the name of Easy. And you definitely hit a key-note."

"What you mean by that?"

"Easy was the one who robbed one of our spots for 40 kilos of pure heroin. Not only that the word is out he's on the feds' payroll."

"Why are you just now informing me of this?"

"I saw no need to bother you with a problem I'd could handle myself."

"Don Pomlerro! Do not screw around with me! If you have not taken the necessary steps to quash a rodent! I'd suggest that you do!!"

"With all do respect. A trap is all ready in place for this rodent!"

"Good. I'm giving you two weeks to report back to me with some good news."

"Don't worry, Mr. Wesley. You will have your good news."

"I'm not the one to worry, Don Pomlerro!"

I'd just woke up from a night of full fledge fucking! And now I'm craving a burger and some fries with plenty of ketchup on top. One of my freaky ass clients has been hitting my phone all morning like it ain't no tomorrow...

What the hell does the good Mayor want now? I'd thought I gave him all he could handle a few hours ago, but apparently not. If this chick got eyes, I know damn well his wife got to be thinking something. Right? But knowing him, he doesn't care what she thinks. He's the Mayor. Right?

But for now, I'm going to ignore him and get myself something to eat before I pass out, you feel me?

Hold up! Wait a damn minute: now! I can't catch a break. This doorbell is giving me the blues right now.

"Richie Rich! What's your problem? Have you forgot how to use a phone?"

"C'mon, Doll Baby, forget about that and let me in."

"If you ain't got a burger and some fries, this better be damn good!"

"Doll Baby, we got a real problem! And I feel it's about time you think about switching lanes!!"

"What are you talking about? Switching lanes?"

The only thing I'm switching is this left-to-right hook if don't make your point!

Richie Rich's eyes indicated that something serious was going on and it was no time for me to be messing around...

"You got to forget about this hoe game and jump on board with me."

"Where is this coming from?"

"You already know where it's coming from! You said it yourself we gotta do something about Don Pomlerro. This fool have gone crazy!

"What you mean gone crazy?"

"He's ready to kill everything in sight, including you. He heard the Crips and Bloods have taken over his operations in West Dallas. Not only that he want to smash the gas on Easy."

"So why do you think he wants me dead?"

"Because he know you got a lot of ties with a lot of people, including the Crips and Bloods."

"So when you think he's going to try and knock me off?"

"Right after you help him to kill Easy."

"In his crazy mind he believe you got a thing for Easy. And with that tleing said, you'll a danger to him!"

"What gave him the idea that Easy |ts a fed rat?"

"One of his goons said le saw Easy leaving ait the federal

building talking to a fed agent."

"Did he say who the agent was?"

"No."

"I think it's time we ask Easy about it?"

"Have you ever got down with Don Pomlerro?"

"No. But I'd can tell you this. I never met a stud that I couldn't break!"

"It sound like to me you are real sure of yourself?"And the only

thing I'm sure of right now the man want us all dead!"

"Assuming you'll right, we got no time to play around! We got to

move!"

"I'm not assuming anything! I'd know what I'm saying it: And do you

realize what you are saying? We got to move now?"

"Hell yeah! I know what I am saying!"

"Let me give you a friendly reminder on a few things. Don Pomlerro

ain't

your average drug dealer. The boy got big feets in the game! Knocking

his

noodles loos is not going to be an easy thing to do!"

"Okay smart guy. So tell me how we gonna play it?"

"Thats why I'd asked you have you ever got down with the man? The

way

I see it you gotta lay the cream on extra thick to the point he doesn't

want

to kill you. In other words, you got to win his confidence...

"T knew it was something else. I'd liked about you besides your

money."

"Oh yeah? And what might that be?"

"Its like playing chess. Richie Rich is always thinking 2 or 3 moves ahead of the game."

"Don't be modest Doll Baby because you do the same damn thang!"

"Maybe. And maybe not. But one thing we do agree on is that a black widow must surface."

Time is definitely not on our side. That's for sure. For the past 6 weeks there have been a straight up blood bath flowing-in the-city! The streets of West Dallas has become a war zone and a killing field for the Crips and Bloods who have consolidated together against the (Chieftain) Don Pomlerro. Just last week alone, between the Crips and Bloods, 15 gang members died, along with 9 members from Don Pomlerro's organization. The ongoing assault from both sides is leaving the city with an outcry demanding for Mayor Driswall to do something concerning this issue or turn in his resignation. It's been well over a month since I've been in contact with Don Pomlerro, which is leaving me wondering when is he going to make his move? And just like Richie Rich said. It's not going to be an easy look to get at Pomlerro. The guy is well protected for sure! The not knowing has gotten me all tensed up. Oh what a feeling...

Damn, I'd forgot to check on them pills I just got from that crazy ass doctor!

These pills look like they ain't about to do a damn thang! I'm going to put about 3 or 4 in my pocket just in case. That freaky ass doctor Sterlings sho got the hots for me. A plus in my favor. Holy shit! Somebody just shot up in the crib

"Come on out, Doll Baby! The Don is waiting to see you."

Oh fuck! Could this be the end of me? What a way to end such a beautiful career. Now, in the famous words of Fred Sanford: Well, momma, I'm coming to join you honey...

When I made it inside the home of Don Pomlerro, he was seated in his large love seat staring right at me with an unfamiliar stare.

"Please have a seat, Doll Baby."

"Have a seat, my ass! What the hell is wrong with you! Having these clowns to shoot up in my crib?"

"I had to get your attention."

"Now that you got it! What the hell do you want with me?"

"Good job, gentlemen. I think I can handle it from here...

"Doll Baby, I'd would like for you to follow me to my bedroom."

"I see you got a lot of damn nerves to be asking me to follow you any-where!"

"Okay. What can I do to make it up to you?"

"T don't know because I can't think right now. That shot made my nerves

go bad!"

"Please follow me."

"Okay. But don't try to pull some bullshit over on me!"

"You is quite stunning when you are angry."

"Flattery gets you nothing here, Don Pomlerro."

"Let me be the judge of that beautiful lady."

This fool didn't waste no time with the move. When we stepped foot inside his mammoth-sized bedroom, he slapped the hell out of me. Landing me on the king-size bed.

"Have you lost your damn mind! What do you call yourself doing?"

"Getting prepared to make love to you!"

Right then, I felt I had to move quick! Because I'd could see the demonic

spirit inside the eyes of this animal!

"With all due respect, Don Pomlerro, to make love doesn't consist of brute force."

"I know that. But there are certain things that turns me on before I start making love."

"I feel what you are saying sir. But just know, there is a first time for everything."

"What you mean?"

"Give me a minute to go to the bathroom, and when I come back, I will show you, what it mean, to truly make love!"

"Hurry up! I can't wait to see it!"

When I came out of the bathroom, I was in my birthday suit, smelling like a fresh rose. Pomlerro was all over my body like a starving dog who haven't eaten in months. When I grabbed him by the face I begin to lick him all over. And within 2 to 3 minutes, Don Pomlerro was dead... I guess you could say that greed kills...

Chapter 9:
Down Goes Richie Rich

Since the death of Don Pomlerro, the city has been rather quiet. There haven't been much talk openly in the matter concerning his death. Now, behind closed doors, well, that's a different subject.

Those silly ass goonies who worked for the man weren't the sharpest tools in the shed. When Don Pomlerro told them they could go because he could handle things from here, those clowns literally left him there all alone...

So being a good girl, I just got my things and left. There was nothing left for me to do. Poor Don Pomlerro, he no longer needed me. What a shame! I felt like he didn't care much for my services anymore...

While I was sitting over here at the trap, the word was spreading on the block like mayo that Don Pomlerro is dead! The whole city is in an uproar! This shit is bigger than I thought. A lot bigger! And the cold thing about it is, Doll Baby got her ass in the mix of all this crap! Here it is, I got a ton of work out there right now, and this lying low shit ain't gonna cut it!

One thing about this situation that bothers me is the fact that I have caught some real feelings for Doll Baby. And to be honest, I don't know if that's bad or good! But what I do know is this. My name is ringing loud in some very different circles. And that's not a good look for me! Damn! I gotta go grab the strap. Somebody is trying to break the door all the way down!

"Man! Get your butt in here. What the hell is wrong with you beating on the door like that? I could have shot the shit outta you boi!"

"Yo, Playboy! It's been a lot of talk that the set is in real trouble with Bon Pomlerro!"

"Have you been drinking, Easy? You know damn well Don Pomlerro is dead!"

"I know that, and you know that. But do Don Pomlerro know that?"

"Easy, I do believe you been drinking this morning for real!"

Either give me a righteous spill or take your ass in the back and go to sleep!"

"I know you think I'm talking crazy but I'm not. Something is going on, Richie Rich, and I'm not talking statement of fact. I'm talking big facts! The Pomlerro crew is saying the Don said this and the Don said that. What? Have the man been raised from the dead?"

"I don't know what is going on but we got to find out fast!"

"You right about that, my guy, and I'm gonna give you another reason why? Do you know that crazy ass nigga Tweezy from Longview?"

"Yeah, I know 'em. He use to work for Don Pomlerro back in the gap."

"Right. Now dig this. Somebody done sent for hia 'eogay ES come to the city for a real reason! You know, like I do this cat ain't the playing type! When he is summoned to an area, something serious is going on for sho!"

"And you'll right! And now that Don Pomlerro is dead, somebody still wanna bust a move on us!"

"But who can it be?"

"That's the million question. If we knew the answer to that, we sure wouldn't be sitting here and that's big facts!"

"You know what I think?"

"Tell me.

"I think it's time we let big Unc in on this one."

"Damn Easy, I forgot all about A.D. You know, back in the gap, the man had big mob ties that brought a lot of wealth to the city."

"Sho you right. It was the boy Dago who put'em all the way on. And when he made it up a lot of people ate from his plate, including us."

"What you mean including us?"

"We were Shorty's back then. Think about it. It was big Unc who set the tone for the dope game being the way that it is now. The prices is so good now our profits have blew through the roof over the past 5 years. And its all because of big Unc!"

"That's his work for sho. Still I hate he's no longer in the game!"

"To lose his only son broke his spirit in half. I remember that shit like it was yesterday! Lil D. was on his ten speed doing what he always do, cracking jokes. The boy just turned 16, feeling himself like we all do. So many young girls was all around Lil D., loving his performance. One girl broke into him and stuck an inch of tongue down his throat. Lil D. was so caught up in what he was doing his didn't see the late blue model Suburban pull up next to him. And the next thing you know, the nigga on the passenger side jumps out and splash Lil D. brains all over the streets! And that's when A.D.'s whole world changed.

"I don't think I ever got the low down on why they'd killed his son?"

"The word was out that Big Unc was moving to much work, and some major players wanted in. And when Big Unc refused to let them in, they set an example real fast!"

"We got to get a Big Unc. The man knows everything that goes down in this city."

"Do you think Big Unc done got down with Doll Baby?"

"I think you should be asking him that."

"So what is wrong with me asking you? You act like you got some feelings

for Doll Baby?"

"I got as much feelings for Doll Baby as you do Slick!"

"I be damn! You do got it bad for Doll Baby!"

"Do you mind if we get back to the business?"

"So what you got in mind?"

"Have you been listening to anything I've been saying to you, son?"

"You know I be listening!"

"I need for you to go ahead and set up a meeting with A.D. as soon as possible."

"Okay. I'm on it."

"Be careful out there, Easy."

"Don't worry about me. I'm good, big homie."

I hope my guy is tight! These streets ain't safe right now. Anybody can get it!

Right now my lil man Easy is a live wire for sho! Don't get it twisted tho. He's a real money getter who is not playing with the full deck!

Hopefully, today will be a good day for me. I got a meeting with this jive ass Mayor Driswall! He talks like somebody is about to bust his ass up! Hell if you ask me the clown deserve whatever he gets! Let me turn this up. I be damn! Old Mayor Driwall wants to crack down on the drug operations in West Dallas. Now I'm wondering is that what he want to talk to me about? I don't know why this broad Carla keeps sending me these pics. She's not my type at all! And besides that, rumor has it she had her last boyfriend set to be robbed, not knowing he was going to be killed during the robbery. That alone is a turn-off for me. I gotta call Easy so we can relocate these bricks...

With all these killings going on my price for a chicken just shot to 32.

If anybody got a problem with it, oh well! The game is just what it is.

"Come on in here boi. I was just about to call you."

"You know I had to come and check on the homie."

"What's in the sack?"

"What it look like crazy man? It's Mickey Playboy!

"You must had me in mind? I'm hungry as hell jack! Now hand it over before I snap!"

"Sho you right. Guess who I drilled last night?"

"Who?"

"Beside Doll Baby, she's slicker than a pan of hot grease"!

"With that being said, only one name comes to mind (Devin)."

"You know it."

"Is she still with that busta?"

"Nah. I don't think so. But any way my nig, hurry up and down that crap! We gotta move!"

One thing I can say about my guy Easy, he always got my back. Its good to know that in times like these, you got someone you can depend on.

As I was headed out the door, Easy shouted out he had to use the bathroom. I told him the same thing he told me to hurry up! When I finally made it out the door, I stood for a few minutes just admiring my brand new Macima sitting on 22's with the fresh candy paint (Royal Blue). Those rims of mine were shining brighter than a 14-carat gold teeth.

Dam! Here I go again. Dropping these damn keys! With all this fluid on my right leg, bending my knees is not a good look for me. But you can bet your ass I'm taking my time to pick 'em up! I knew it, I knew it! A damn cramp in my back! Every day in the hood something always bring about a new situation. It wasn't a cramp that Richie Rich caught in the back; it was two slugs from a Glock .40 that dropped him to the pavement. And in his confused mind, he never heard the sound that closed his eyes...   In this game, no one seems to play by the book! The bright clouds over his head seemed to suggest: DOWN GOES RICHIE RICH...

Chapter 10:
Don Pomlerro

This Mr. Wesley is all over my damn nerves! Hell! I can't even take a crap without his nose being stuck up my ass! Speaking of the devil, he's ringing the doorbell right now!

"Come on in, Mr. Wésley."

"Thank you so much, Doll Baby. It's rather cool out tonight.”

"Yes, it is. Can I offer you something to drink, Mr. Wesley?"

"That's mighty kind of you. Yes."

Okay. What will it be?

"I will take a glass of your best champagne."

“Coming right up."

"Doll Baby, I got a question for you."

"Ask your question, Mr. Wesley."

“After all these years, why do you still call me Mr. Wesley?"

"I don't know Mr. Wesley. And to be honest with you, sir, I never gave

it much thought."

"Doll Baby, I'm inclined to believe that you and I have a special relationship going on between us."

"Ycs, Mr. Wesley, I can see that."

"I don't think you do."

"Why do you say that?"

"You know damn well why I'm saying it!"

"I don't know what your problem is, sir, but I think you need to explain yourself!"

"No! I'm not the one to be doing the explaining. It's you, Doll Baby!"

"Mr. Wesley, I don't have a clue into what you are talking about right now!"

"I see you got it bad when it comes to spinning someone."

"I'm tired of the cat and mouse game, so make your point now!"

"Alright, Doll Baby. Here it is. Who was that young man I saw you going inside the hotel with?"

"Mr. Wesley, you must have forgotten what my profession is?"

"I have not forgotten a damn thing you little tramp! Especially when you break a date with me just to be with someone else!"

Oh my God! I forgot all about the date I had with Mr. Wesley. It's no wonder the man is tripping!

"Mr. Wesley, you got to forgive me on this one because I honestly forgot all about our date."

"By you saying that, you think that will make it right?"

"I didn't say it for that reason. I said it because that's the truth. Anyway, Why is you so upset about it?"

"Are you freaking blind! Have you not notice I'm in love with your black ass!"

"But why Me. Wesley? Why have you fallen in love with me? You know who I am and what I am. I'm not the one for you to be falling in love with!"

"Stop this foolish talk, Little girl! The damage is already done. And from this day forward, you are going to fly right or reap the consequences!"

"Is you threatening me Mr. Wesley?"

"No Doll Baby. It's no threat. Just stating the facts that's all!"

"Who in the hell do you think you'll talking to like that! You should already know this type of crap just don't fly with me!" |

"Young lady, I think it may be time for you to check my resume."

"Whatever you mean by that I could care less! And as a matter of fact, it's time for you to leave, Mr. Wesley."

"Of course, Doll Baby. Oh, by the way, you might want to go and check on your friend. I think he may be calling for you..."

In some weird sort of way, Mr. Wesley appears to be a dangerous man. What did he mean about check on your friend?

This was the day of Don Pomlerro's funeral. His casket was pearl white, trimmed in gold. Inside the funeral home surrounding the casket of Don Pomlerro were large stem roses inside of many different beautiful vases. The atmosphere was rather quiet. The crowd of people were moving in silence while attempting to take their seats. When the funeral of Don Pomlerro had come to an end everybody preceded to head on over to the grave-site...

Right after Don Pomlerro was laid to rest, that's when the whispers started. You could see different people moving in different directions while being engaged in their own conversation. Now there were two men who stood out amongst the crowd, standing next to a black Escalade with their hands inside their pockets.

"You know, my friend, I hate we had to meet under such difficult circumstances."

"The feeling is mutual, my friend."

"After things have calmed down, we have a lot to talk about."

"Yes. I would like to set up a meeting with you no later than tomorrow."

"T will meet with you at your place, say around noon?"

"Of course, my friend."

Meanwhile, all over West Dallas, the word is out that Richie Rich has been killed. There, Doll Baby was sitting at home watching the local news as they gave details into the shooting of Richie Rich. The pain she was feeling right now was causing her to have a massive headache. Not realizing what she was feeling at the moment. This disturbing news has caused Doll Baby to have chills all over her body, knowing she could be next to be taken out of the game...

"But it won't be today, and you can bet the bank on it!"

The two hundred thousand dollar poodle (Silva) made her present known as her master made it to the. front of the door,

"Come right in, my friend. I see you are right on time as always."

"I would not have it any other way."

"What would you like to drink?"

"Nothing. Let's get right down to business!"

"Yes. Of course."

"What I propose is that we hit'em all at once!"

"Including Doll Baby?"

"Yes. Including Doll Baby."

"I'd was wondering when you were going to snap back and realize a snake head must come off! So this is what's going to happen in a month from row. I will send some of my people to negotiate a deal with the Crips and Bloods.

"What makes you so sure you can pull it off?"

"I will give them an offer they'd won't be able to refuse. And in the meantime, stay close to Doll Baby and drill all the information you can out of her concerning that creep Driswall! He has something very valuable that belongs to me...

"I'm on it, Don Pomlerro."

Chapter 11:
Sweet Dreams Doll Baby

Today is one of them days when Life is treating me kinda bad! All this crap coming down on me has left a stain on my rep! And the way I'm feeling about handling it a lot of folks ain't gonna like it! All my life I had to grind hard for mine, and I refuse to let anybody take my grind from me!

Whatever is going on in this city, they'd got me in the mix of all this mess! It's not my fault these lame ass men got the hots for me, and most of their old ladies look at me sideways, knowing that many of them want a piece of me too!

Doorbell ringing.

"Come on in, Mayor Driswall.""You look terrible, man!"

"I feel just like I look, Doll Baby."

"Can I get you something, Mayor?"

"No thanks, Doll Baby. I just need to talk with you right now."

"Okay, Mayor. Start talking."

"You see, Doll Baby, several years ago, when I'd first started my campaign on the road to becoming the Mayor of this city, my campaign was funded by the biggest drug lord on this side of the earth! And I think you know him very well. Or should I say, you use to know him very well?"

"Anyway. Don Pomlerro paid me good money for years to make sure his operations ran smoothly throughout West Dallas. You see, a couple of months ago myself and Mary Lou (My wife) were invited to this large gala event at the (ATS§T STADIUM) in honor of Texas's very own Senator, Mel Calvert. Now at this event I'd was the last to speak and I could not wait until thing was over!"

"Once me and Mary Lou made our way inside the V.I.P. area I saw something that immediately caught my attention. I'd seen a man whose name was spoken in different circles connected to the community. With that being said, why would he be having a conversation with Don

Pomlerro? That was the million-dollar question? In my mind, I had to get to the bottom of what was going on between them two. So instead of me making an appointment with Pomlerro, I decided just to barge into his office a couple days later. And guess who was in the office with him?"

"The guy with the high-ranking status in the community?"

"Bingo! When I rushed in unannounced, the guy turned from talking with Pomlerro looked directly at me, not even realizing he had dropped something on the floor. He told Pomlerro he would talk with him later. And when he walked passed me, he gave a nod, and left. Without hesitation, I pulled up a chair close to Pomlerra's desk where the object was lying still...

"One could look in Pomlerro's eyes to know he was very upset with me.

And the conversation went something like this:

"I don't recall me giving you an invite at this time Mayor?"

"No, you did not, Don Pomlerro."

"So then why are you here unannounced?"

"I guess my curiosity has gotten the best of me."

"Just cut through the red tape, Mayor, and make your point!"

"Alright, Don Polerro. My senses tell me I smell a rat! And since I'm The Mayor of this city and you are a close associate of mine, I'd got the right to know what is the connection between you and the gentleman who just left your office."

Small beads began to pop up all over Polerro's forehead. I knew right then I'd just hit a major nerve!

"Mayor you are a man of great understanding I do assume? You have been around the playing field for a very long time. So, what I'm about to say now you will have no problem comprehending the message. Stop sticking that fat ass nose of yours into things that don't concern you!! And another thing my friend you need to keep in mind."

"And what might that be?"

"You are still on the payroll!"

"You know something Don Pomlerro?"

"No. Tell me."

"Let me share with you the difference between myself and those other clowns who work for you! They're afraid of you Pomlerro, I'm not! And when I'd ask a question I demand an answer!"

"Good Mayor Driswall. Do you recall a conversation we once had several weeks ago concerning how much weight you wanted to lose?"

"Yes. I remember the conversation."

"Well consider it done! Now get the hell up out of my office!!"

I intentionally drop my glasses to the floor so that I'd could retrieve the object. After placing it inside my right pant pocket I'd got up wishing Pomlerro a good day and left...

"Now that you got my mind racing there is three things I wanna know. Number one: "Why come to me with all of this?"

"You see, Doll Baby, you are the only one that I trust. Along with the fact that I'm in love with you."

"Are you serious, Mayor?"

"We can't focus on that right now, sweetheart. We got bigger problems to consider."

"The second thing I wanna know what was the object that you found?"

"It was a thumb drive."

"A thumb drive?"

"Yes, Doll Baby, a thumb drive."

"Do you care to share with me what is on that drive?"

"First of all, what is on that thumb drive definitely is not good. Not good at all."

"Cut the crap, Mayor! What is on that damn drive that got you all shook up!"

"I'm going to give you the opportunity to see it all for yourself. And for whatever reason somebody wanted your life spared, Doll Baby!"

"Now I need for you to explain that one for me?"

"Like I said, you will know a lot once you see it for yourself."

"Alright, Mayor. Now for my final question. The man you saw talking with Don Pomlerro, do you know him?"

"We both do Doll Baby."

"So, do you mind telling me who it is?"

"No, I don't mind."

This mess happened so fast it felt like I was losing my damn mind! A cloud of smoke filled the room with the smell of toxic chemicals that were slowly driving me unconscious. And now I'm having a hard time breathing. It seemed like time was slipping away from me real fast! Before falling to the floor, my head was pounding harder than a punch from Mike Tyson as I drifted off into unconsciousness.

And when I woke up there, I was lying in a hospital bed with cops all around just staring at me with that hungry ass look in their eyes! It was that fat homicide detective, Fat Burt, who approached me. A Fat Joe wanna be is what the people say about'em. But anyway, here comes the bull jive...

"Hello Doll Baby? Even in a hospital bed, you still look damn good! Oh, by the way, why didn't you come to see a few weeks ago? I'd guess my money don't spend hah?"

"You can cut the shit, Fat Burt! And state your reason for being here!"

"I think you already know why I'm here."

"I don't know a damn thing until you tell me! You got that!"

"My, my, my. Did I spark a flame inside your horny ass Doll Baby?"

"I knew it was something that I'd liked about you, Fat Burt."

"I can't wait to hear it."

"I'd like it when you can keep your damn mouth closed!"

"Well, we know that ain't going to happen any time soon. But anyway, let's get back to the business at hand. What I wanna know is what happened in that house between you and Mayor Driswall? And don't give me no sassy lip Doll Baby!"

"Forget that! What me and Mayor had going on is none of your damn business!"

"Did I not tell you I didn't want to hear none of your sassy lip service!"

"Well, you heard it!"

"If you think I'm here playing games with you, lady, you are highly mistaken! If you don't want me to bust your ass right now I think you'd better start talking!"

"It's time that you tell me what the hell is going on!"

"Alright, Doll Baby, I'll play your little game with you. How did the Mayor end up with a hole on the right side of his temple the size of a fucking quarter! Do you care to explain that to me?"

How does this clown expect me to explain something I don't have no knowledge of?

"Fat Burt, I'm gonna give it to you straight. The only thing I remember before passing out was asking the Mayor a question."

"Okay Doll Baby that's a start. Now will you be so kind and inform me what was the question you asked the mayor and why?"

"Right now I can't answer that because I don't remember."

"Doll Baby, I'm going to get Mack with you within the week. And I'm telling you right now you better start remembering something...

I know for sho I gotta get up outta here A.S.A.P.!!!

Today, a question was raised in the minds of so many people. Will the sun stop shining on Richie Rich? There he was in the hospital, where the doctors were performing major surgery on him as they'd realized one of the bullets that was lodged in his spine had done serious damage to his spinal cord. Once again, could this be the end of Richie Rich?

Meanwhile, downstairs, inside the waiting room, sits (Barefoot) Richie Rich's moms, Easy, and A.D.. Barefoot looks over at A.D. and Easy with a look of desperation in her eyes...

"I don't know why you two is looking at me sideways! Like you don't know what's going on! But one of all needs to be telling me what happened to my baby boy!"

A.D. looks at Barefoot and says in a mellow tone:

"Barefoot, we're just as confused as you, and that's real!"

"I know you know something, Easy? He was with you when the bullshit went down!"

"Just like I'd told those cops Barefoot, when I had finished using the bathroom, I went outside, and there was Richie Rich lying on the pavement face down."

"Nigga! What you'll telling me that's all you know?"

"Just that simple, Barefoot. That's all I know for sho!"

"I can't believe this crap! My boy is fighting for his life and nobody knows a damn thing!"

"We got to chill on fighting amongst ourselves and find out who did this to your son, Barefoot?"

"Okay, Mister A.D. where do we start?"

"I think our best bet is to start with Doll Baby."

"Man, is you serious? Do you know how many times I've come close to removing this bread from the earth? Hell! That bitch done drunk too much of that lead water for real!"

"So, what you think about it, Easy?"

"I'm with you A.D.. We gotta start with Doll Baby."

"Why is you two so dead set on Doll Baby? What ya'll know that I don't know?"

"You see, Barefoot, what happened to your son had a direct connection to Doll Baby."

"Meaning?"

"Meaning that Doll Baby been playing around in a very big playing field with some major players. And one of those players was Don Pomlerro."

"I'd thought he was dead?"

"Sho you right. Now, before Pomlerro died, you gotta remember he had beef with the Crips and Bloods. And don't be blind-sided. Because everybody who is somebody knows your son is a powerful member of the Crips who is moving a lot of work throughout West Dallas. But you already know that Barefoot, since you are a team player. But anyway. When Pomlerro found out that the Crips and Bloods had a tight grip on his operations in West Dallas, especially the Crips. He sent for Doll Baby to help him get rid of your son!"

"So that is why Richie is in the hospital? all shot up? Because of this tramp!"

"How'd could that be Barefoot? When Don Pomlerro himself is dead?

"So, what is you saying, A.D.? A ghost shot my son?"

"Not at all."

"Just tell me what you know."

"At this point, I can only speculate."

"Well start speculating then!"

"Did you know your son had ties with Don Pomlerro?"

"No, I didn't."

"Well, he did. And here's the thing. One of Pomlerro's stash spots got hit for 40 bricks. He later learned that it was Easy who made the play. A couple of his goons lay on Easy, watching his every move. For whatever reason, Don Pomlerro believed Easy was a federal informant. And when he started gathering information on Easy, he found out how tight your son, Easy, and Doll Baby were. Now in his mind Pomlerro assumed all three was in on the play for the 40 bricks."

"Okay, let me ask Easy something."

"What you wanna know, Barefoot?"

"Is you a fed rat?"

"I'm a lot of things Barefoot, but that ain't one of 'em for sho!"

"Listen at this Barefoot. This is the flee flicker. Instead of Pomlerro killing Doll Baby he wanted her help because he had hidden feeling for her."

"Easy, how tight was you three?"

"I don't know what you mean Barefoot."

"You know damn well what I mean! Did you and my son have feelings for this slut!"

"I can't speak for Richie Rich, Barefoot, but I do have feelings for Doll Baby."

"So, you don't know if my son have feelings for this woman?"

"No, I can't, Barefoot."

"Now that Pomlerro is dead. Someone else has taken his place. Someone more ruthless than he could ever be!"

"Damn the suspense, A.D., who is this mutha!"

"Adonis Pomlerro. The brother of the late Don Pomlerro…

The rain have been pouring down all day while I've been standing out front of the hospital catching a chill waiting on my girl Shine to come and scoop me up. And just like clockwork, the girl is right on time...

"Come on in here, girl friend, before you catch a damn cold!"

"Sho you right! I can damn near feel it coming on."

"Let's just get to my place A.S.A.P."

It was something different about my girl Shine for real. I don't know what it is, but I do know something is different about her...

"Let me help you up outta here, Doll Baby?"

"I do appreciate it, Shine, but I got this. And don't be pulling that pity shit on me either!"

"Cut it out boo! You know it ain't like that. But what would be a good idea tho if you went upstairs and took a hot showers."

"Yea, I could do that."

Shine was right. The shower did me good. Trying to piece all this mess together done gave me a serious headache! All I wanna do now is just lie back and chill for a minute...

"Look! Didn't I tell you a shower would bring you all the way back?"

"You did, girlfriend."

"Check this? I'm gonna whip up something for you to eat. And while I'm doing that, give me the spill on what happened at your crib.”

"It happened so fast, Shine. I'd couldn't even think straight for real!"

“Why don't you just start at the beginning?” Do you need a couple of Tylenols or something?"

"No. I'm cool on that. But anyway, Mayor Griswall comes by the crib with this scary ass look on his face! He comes in talking of stuff at first that wasn't making much sense to me. When he handed me that thumb drive, he gave me some of the spill but not all of it.”

"I don't understand what you'll. saying?"

"What I'm saying is this! The man told me bits and pieces of the story, and the rest I could find out about on the thumb drive.”

"So did you have time to look at it?"

"Not yet. But you can bet this! I'm on it."

"You already know these big shots is in an uproar over this man's death?"

"You know I know that."

"Until they'd can get some answers, you know they'd coming at 'cha Doll Baby!"

"And now that I have had some time to think, how could I not know that? They'd coming to see about that in full force!"

"So what you gonna do about it?"

"When I get all rested up, I'm going to see what's on that thumbdrive. And whatever is on there, it cost the Mayor his life."

"And with that knowledge, it could cost you yours!"

"Well, we just got to wait and see."

"This ain't funny Doll Baby!"

"And I'm not taking it there either!"

"Your Life is on the damn line! You know that? Do you care about anything I'm saying to you?"

"Right now I don't won't to think. I'd just wanna chill and relax and listen to some mellow music on the real."

"Doll Baby. What do you want?"

"What you mean what I'd want?"

"In life, what is it that you truly want for yourself?"

"What I want right now is to be left alone!"

"Even from me, girlfriend?"

"Even from you, Shine."

"Just give me a minute, I'll be out of your way. But first you gotta and drink what I made for you, sugar."

"You know I'd got no problem with that."

One thing I can say about Shine, the girl can cook her ass off! Whoa! feeling woozy., Damn! What did Shine put in that wine?

Don't worry about that! Sweet dreams, Doll Baby... When you wake up gonna feel Shine's love all over you...

Chapter 12:
Ripped Apart

As you begin to read this chapter, allow me to properly introduce myself. My name is Pomlerro. Adonis Pomlerro, the brother of the late Don Pomlerro. Tonight I am seated in my home with a dear friend of mine. Don't ever think, dear readers, that I'm a rude man , but I got to get back to the business at hand...

"Mister Tweezy? How do you like your champagne?"

"Like always, Don Pomlerro, it's the best in town."

"Yes, I agree. I would like to commend you for the good work you put in for me."

"No need to commend me, Don Pomlerro. The work was not a problem. In fact, the pleasure was all mine."

"Good. Now what are we going to do about that A.D, fellow?"

"What about 'em?"

"I'd know you have heard how he's been slandering the Pomlerro's name?"

"A.D. is old now. I can't see him being a problem, especially after what happened to his son."

"Mister Tweezy. I'd thought you knew me better than that?"

"What you saying, Don Pomlerro?"

"When have you ever known me to take chances?"

"You don't."

"That's right. I don't! I'm nothing like my older brother. As strong as he was, he took too many chances. He possessed a weakness when it came down to certain people. A weakness I don't possess! I want them all dead!!! You got that?"

"Loud and clear, Don Pomlerro."

"So what about that Richie Rich? Have he stopped breathing yet?"

"That I don't know."

"And why not?"

"Because that wasn't my work. If that was my work, you wouldn't have to ask about."

"Yes, I'd have to agree. So why don't you make it your work? Making it a top priority on your to-do list?"

"Say less! I'm on it like yesterday."

"I'd need to ask you something?"

"I'm listening."

"It seems to me like that Doll Baby chick got a lot of people caught up in her web. Now tell me? Are you one of those people, Mister Tweezy?"

"Instead of me telling it to you, I'm gonna show it to you!"

"You couldn't have said it any better than that. But still we are in a very difficult situation."

"Meaning?"

"Meaning the city councils have appointed an assistant mayor to our fair city. And I assure you, this lady is nothing to be playing around with!"

"Whats her name?"

"Francis Duberry."

"You talking about D.A. Duberry?"

"One and the same! The same one who sent me on my first journey mister Tweezy. And let me make myself perfectly clear! This woman is going to be a real problem for us in the long run."

"The way I'd see it, Don Pomlerro, before looking too deep into this Duberry chick we gotta start tightening up all loose ends starting with Doll Baby and Richie Rich!"

Don Pomlerro looked away with a puzzled look m his face wondering how much could he trust Tweezy? Most of the blacks that Don Pomlerro had dealings with over the years, one thing he definitely knew about most of them they'd would sell out their own benefactors for a piece of change…

You got to remember that this Don is nothing like his brother. But to some degree, he is. Adonis Pomlerro is more ruthless and dangerous than the other one! He lives without a conscious!

"Mister Tweezy, I'd think this may be a good time if you head on down to the airport and pick up my assistant."

"And who might this assistant be?"

"Let's just say, it would be in your best interest to guard her with your life!"

The last thing I'd remembered was Shine drilling me about the Mayor Driswall. Don't you know when I went to use the bathroom, I found dried up cum all over my pussy and thighs! I know I don't get down like that. So, what happened? I'll tell you what happened. That got damn Shine! That bitch put something in my drink and did her thing with me, knowing I don't play that shit! What I'd know, she got me twisted for real! All the bull jive that's going on in my life, and she wanna pull this shit! I knew the tramp had a thing for me, but I didn't know she would take it this far!

Now, when I'd think back to a month ago when we where at my crib getting high Shine stated to me that she loved me. I didn't pay no attention to what she said. I was just enjoying my high. But I guess the girl is for real to go through all this trouble to get at me. I don't care how for real she is! I'm going to get myself together so I can kick off into that ass…

Over on Rupert Circle, at one of their hangout spots, the Rupert Circle Crips had a serious meeting going down with Easy leading the way. The moods inside were very disturbing for some of the gang members. Now Baby Q was not liking a damn thing he was hearing! Everyone inside could feel the tension brewing in the air.

"Yo! I called this meeting because we got some big problems headed our way."

Now, Baby Q was not a baby by far. In fact, he's the number one hitter in their crew.

"Forget the beat around cuz. Just drop it on a dime!"

"Sho you right, Baby Q. Check it. The boy Don Pomlerro put a stiff order out to kill all the Crips and Bloods on sight who been messing around with his operations out in West Dallas."

"I'd thought you told us Don Pomlerro was dead?"

"What I told you is the truth. Who I'm talking about is the brother of Don Pomlerro(Adonis). The new Don! And not only that, we got more problems coming from that new assistant Mayor chick! In other words, we gotta kill two birds at the same time!"

"Okay my guy. How we gonna bust a move like that?"

"The hype is they'd got something major going on downtown this week. Now with that being said, I'm going to set a play where we can take 'em both at the same time. Don't worry, Playboy, the play is A one!"

"It better be! Because you know like me this clown want our heads on the chopping block for real!"

"Don't trip, just follow the move."

Four days later, Doll Baby gets a call from Easy informing her who was responsible for the work done on Richie Rich...

Baby Q was sitting in a green Chevy, ducked off, waiting for the Assistant Mayor and Don Pomlerro to come out of the Convention Center (Downtown Dallas). The 40 caliber was in position to do some major damage! Easy constructed Baby Q to make sure he hit the assistant first. And that's just what he did! The bullets from that carbine had a mind of their own while ripping her apart! People everywhere were screaming and running all over the place, trying to shield themselves. For a brief moment, Baby Q took his eyes off Don Pomlerro. And when he re-positioned himself, Don Pomlerro was nowhere in sight...

Slowly creeping in the back field was an unknown figure headed straight for the green Chevy with no approaching sound...

Baby Q must have known the silent figure because he let the window down. The smile on his face was wiped away when he saw that the ugly lord have mercy aimed at his face! And without hesitation, Baby Q never heard the sounds that took his life. Three to the face left him slumped... Ripped apart...

Chapter 13:
The Call For Dale O'Hara

In the city of West Dallas, there have been a public outcry concerning the deaths of those two public officials! The Governor of Texas had a meeting with every law enforcement agency in the Dallas and Fort Worth area to shed some light on these terrible tragedies...

Commissioner Dan Albright sends for homicide detective Kirt Tillman...

"Come on in here, Tillman! Have a seat. The Powernor have been all over my ass about these killings! So, my question to you is, what is you and your office doing to solve these murders?"

"To be honest, Commissioner, the only thing we have right now is that we'll be waiting on Ballistic to give us a make on what type of weapon those bullets were fired from."

"S,o the kid that was found dead in that car, do you think he was the shooter?"

"I'm sure of it."

"Well answer me this? What makes you so sure this kid is the shooter?"

"I'd just have this gut feeling that's all."

"We don't need no damn gut feeling Tillman! We'd need facts and we need them now!"

"Right now, I don't know what to tell you, Commissioner. We are doing the best we can to come up with some leads. But at this point, we'll just waiting on the ballistic to come through."

"Waiting on ballistic is not good enough! I need results now!"

"Just tell me, sir? What you need from me?"

"At this point nothing! I don't hear nothing concrete coming from you. (EXCUSES) only!"

"Like I'd said, Commissioner. My office is on top of it. We'd just got to wait on ballistic."

"Oh, by the way, there is something I'd need for you to do."

"What is it, sir?"

"I need for you to connect me with the homicide division in Memphis, Tennessee."

"Okay, Commissioner. But why do you want to speak with homicide down in Memphis?"

"Have you ever heard of detective Dale O'Hara?"

Commissioner Dan saw that his words seemed to have gave him pause... Detective Tillman took time studying the look on Commissioner Dan's face before speaking.

"What's wrong, detective? You can't speak?"

"Yes, Commissioner? I'd know who Dale O'Hara is. He's a freaking nightmare!"

"How can you say that about a man who have solved more cases than all of your detectives combined?"

"With all due respect, Commissioner, you and I both know Dale O'Hara is not your average homicide detective. His method for solving cases is not what we do here at our agency. The reputation that Dale O'Hara has acquired over the years seem a little unorthodox."

"Detective Tillman, the Governor of this great State of Texas, is all over my ass like flies on shit! So do you think I'd give a damn about Dale O'Hara's method? Of course I don't! I'm looking for results, and Dale O'Hara is the one to bring me those results. Now connect me to the Memphis Homicide Division."

"Yes, sir."

Today was a pleasant day for Dale O'Hara as he made his way back to his office. Once inside, he saw a light flashing from his lab top. And before looking at the message, he hesitated, thinking it might be good to treat himself with his favorite treat - *A joint of weed...*

What you are about to learn of Dale O'Hara is quite remarkable.

His face has appeared in more newspapers than a bulletin board covered with America's Most Wanted! Apparently, Dale O'Hara is not your average homicide detective. He definitely has a unique way of solving cases. Now smoking weed enhances O'Hara's thinking abilities without a doubt. One of the biggest cases of his career almost went down the drain when he couldn't find any weed for two weeks. The man got so irritated with himself that he stayed in his room for days without calling in on his job...

"Yes. This is Dale O'Hara. What can I do for you?"

"Mister O'Hara your reputation precedes you. Oh, how rude of me Mister O'Hara. Please allow me to properly introduce myself."

"You can just call me Dale if you don't mind?"

"Dale, it is then. Well, Dale, my name is Dan Willingham, the of West Dallas, Texas."

"Okay, Commissioner Willingham. For you to be calling me way down here in Memphis, it's got to be important. So run it down to me?"

"You are quite right, Dale, it's very important. You see the The Governor of our great state is all over my ass concerning two high profile cases that recently happened in our city, Mayor Driswall and Assistant Mayor, Francis Duberry)."

"Yes, I'd saw that on the evening news. But you got to excuse me, Commissioner, I don't think it's necessary at this point to continue to go into details about this. But my question to you is this. Don't they'd have homicide investigators in Texas?"

"Yes, they do."

"In that case, then why are you calling on me?"

"Allow me to give it to you, straight, Mister O'Hara! What has happened in our city, it appears that our detectives is not sufficient enough to handle such a case with this type of magnitude. Now, just about every agency in the south knows that your style of solving cases goes hand in hand with the late great Sherlock Holmes. And for me, that puts you in a class all by yourself, Mister Dale O'Hara."

"Yeah. Well, I don't know about all of that commissioner. It seem like to me you'll trying to mount me up for an instant go."

"I'd guess you can say that. And the truth of the matter is simply this. We'd need your assistance down here, Dale, and whatever you need, you will be accommodated."

"Before I'd can make a move like that, sir, I got to run it by my boss."

"Don't worry about that, O'Hara. Everything has already been arranged."

"Boy! You don't waste any time, do you, Commissioner?"

"I'm afraid I don't, Detective O'Hara."

I'd told you in the beginning, when I ran off from my parents, I ran into all kinds of mess! And to cap that off, I'd just run into some strange shit a few minutes ago that sho caught my attention! You see. When I pulled up at the hospital, how'd bout I saw Mister Wesley and Easy walking together, headed inside the hospital. For a minute, I was tempted to scream out at both their asses, wondering what the hell they were up to! I had no idea these two even knew each other...

But what I do know something is going on and I'm about to find out just what it is! With slow, calculated steps, moving smooth like a panther, frantically, I had to calm myself when I'd realized where these two were headed with a stupid look on their faces.

Now, you could just imagine how the hairs on the back of my neck were standing up, knowing something just wasn't right... When I'd looked inside Richie Rich hospital room, both Neer Wesley and Easy looked directly into my face as if to say, what the fuck..."What the hell are you doing here!"

"What the hell you mean? What I'm doing here!"

"Cut the crap, Doll Baby! Now, why are you here?"

"Mister Wesley, that is a question I'd should be asking you and Easy! Why is you two standing over Richie's bed like that?"

"I don't think that's none of your business Doll Baby!"

"You can shut the hell up right now, Easy! Richie suppose to be your boy and here it is you'll standing over him, talking crazy to me! I'd want you to tell me right now what you and Mister Wesley got going on!"

"Calm down, Doll Baby. I didn't want to tell you at first because I did not think you would understand. Richie has been in so much pain and these idiot doctors wouldn't give him what he really needed (Morphine), so I went and got it for him."

"Why, Mister Wesley, you could have told me that without being so secret about it."

"Like I'd told you, Doll Baby, I didn' think you would understand."

"Oh, but I do, Mister Wesley. Now I can go home and rest a little, knowing that Richie is in good hands."

"You do that. I will come by later on so we can have a drink or two."

"You do that, Mister Wesley. I'll be waiting."

"Do you think she bought the morphine thing?"

"To be honest with you, son, I don't think she did."

"So, what we gonna do?"

"I'll tell you what we not going to do. We are not going to do what we came here to do. What I'd for you to do right now is to go and keep an eye on that A.D. character."

"Beside keeping an eye on him 'em what else do you want me to do?"

"Nothing!"

"I'm on it."

"Good."

"Right now, when it comes down to those two, I don't believe a damn thing coming out of their mouth! Damn! I just had an ugly thought. What if they'd came here to kill Richie?"

"They can't do it now because they'd know I can link them. But why would they'd want to kill Richie for? It just don't make sense too me..."

"That damn Barefoot don't like me but still I'd got too get somebody over here to look out for Richie. Now who the hell is this beating on my damn window!"

"Yes. May I help you?"

"Yes. I'm Detective Dale O'Hara."

"Your badge also say, you are from Memphis?"

"That's true."

"Alright then. Why is you way down here in Texas asking to speak with me?"

"Can we go some place to talk?"

"I don't think so. And besides, I don't know you like!"

"I'm not going to bite your head off! I'd just need a few minutes of your time."

"No! Now leave me alone!"

"One week on the job, and I just got a taste of what they'd talking about concerning this chick. This broad is definitely going to be hard to handle!"

Chapter 14:
Honor, Respect before Death

The thing about me is that I'm going to always be Doll Baby, whether you like it or not! When my parents turned me out to this game, there was no turning back for me! I can't speak for everybody, but I can speak for me. The way I play the game is the way I'd live. And the way I live, I play for keeps! The boy Richie Rich, yeah, I caught a few feelings for 'em, but he doesn't know that. And it's not my place to tell 'em either. . . You may say, What about Easy? The same thing went for him, too. But if I'd find out he's playing foul, it's not gonna be anything nice for sho! Will you just look at all the bull crap that has risen in my life? Mister Wesley, Don Pomlerro, Shine, Easy, Richie Rich, Barefoot, Mayor Driswall, and the list goes on and on…

And with that being said, now I'd got this damn cop on my line who's not from Texas! The roll of the dice got me wondering if the roll is still in my favor? Who knows? Anyway, as I think back to my coming-up days, all I'd wanted to do was break a sucker. Because that's all I'd knew was to break one. . .

You know, there have been several rumors going around saying, Can Doll Baby be tamed? You gotta know I'm not going to answer that for you! And don't think that I have forgotten about that bitch Shine and how she played me because I haven't! When I went looking for her black ass the first time, I couldn't find her! But the second is going to be a charm. . . And what about the new Don? This clown is worst than the first one! That's right, folks. This stupid mutha fucka put the double O in fool! You know he can't wait to rip my head off!

Oh! I'd forgotten about that big dopeboy I knocked off for all that bread! Now dig this? This boy is plugged in good with the crips. Then the word got out that I started a war between the Crips and Bloods…Old Mister Wesley. Now, what part did he play in all of this madness? The only sure thing I'd know about Mister Wesley he's rich and he's in love with me for sho! To be for real. This old cat can't get enough of all this sweet brown sugar… But still, I gotta give it to you straight. You see, the other night, this old man scared the living hell outta me! After getting into a heated argument with him, he looked at me with murder in his eyes and said, "You will not leave me ever!"

Can you imagine Doll Baby being shook up like that? Well, I was! Even when the boy Easy paid for the pussy, his loving was so damn good to me! But like the boss bitch that I am he will never know it… Now, when it comes down to old Mayor Driswall, I feel real bad about him. Damn! Why do I keep forgetting to look at that hard drive? Maybe what's on that drive will shed some light on what happened to Mayor Driswall. . . Now, here I am feeling, just like a bitch with nothing to lose! What a way to feel ha?

You know, for some folks, money didn't seem to matter. But for me, it mattered a lot. But what about now? I'd mean right now? Does the money matter to me? Can it save my life? At this point, I don't think so. In the very beginning, before I'd started telling you my story, I made it clear that I would not change anything about how I came up in this life. But now I don't know about all that! Yeah, it's some things I think I'd change now. . .

In this life, money and murder are the sauce for the day! With sex, hate, and betrayal being the main ingredients… All my life, I've been hard on a trick. And that's why so many of them have fallen in love with me because of the way I'd work it! You can see the greed and lust all over these tricks faces. And given the right opportunity, these clowns would leave their wives and children in a full-fledged mess . . .

The one thing that keeps flowing through my mind is whether or not Easy is a fed rat? Oh well! This bull jive is just too much for me to soak in right now. The only soaking I'm gonna do right now is soak my aching body while I'd smoke on a fat sack of that good exotic weed. Just thinking about it is a real turn on for me…

Just when Doll Baby made it inside the crib, it started thundering and lighting real bad outside. Doll Baby had to pee so bad she dropped her purse and left her door unlocked. When she was done, she went back to lock her door. One wouldn't even know if this girl was afraid of the lighting or not because she didn't show it... Once she made it inside her bedroom, she started searching for that og cush she'd been smoking on all week long...

After finishing off her first joint, Doll Baby stripped down to her birthday suit, looking so fine! There she was, standing in front of her full-length mirror, admiring what she was truly blessed with....

Now, suddenly, without warning, there was a loud burst of thunder that kinda shook Doll Baby for a minute. When she finally got herself back together, looking back into the mirror, she saw a reflection, but the reflection wasn't a reflection of her, but the reflection of a woman standing inside a spider web. Trying to figure out what she was looking at, Doll Baby had a hard time hearing the unknown voice behind her. But when she finally heard it, she definitely didn't like what she heard.

'Don't turn around, Doll Baby! Night, night, you bitch!"

www.ingramcontent.com/pod-product-compliance
Lightning Source LLC
Chambersburg PA
CBHW040839010826
48978CB00012BB/825